A HEART DIVIDED

Life is hard for Anne and her father under Cromwell's harsh rule, which has reduced them from wealth to poverty. When tragedy strikes it looks as if there is no one she can turn to for help. With one friend fearing for his life and another apparently lost to her, a man she hates sees her as a way of fulfilling all his ambitions. Will she have to surrender to him or lose everything?

SHEILA HOLROYD

---◆---

A HEART
DIVIDED

Complete and Unabridged

LINFORD
Leicester

First published in Great Britain in 2008

First Linford Edition
published 2009

British Library CIP Data

Holroyd, Sheila
    A heart divided.—Large print ed.—
Linford romance library
    1. Love stories
    2. Large type books
    I. Title
    823.9'2 [F]

    ISBN 978–1–84782–563–6

Published by
F. A. Thorpe (Publishing)
Anstey, Leicestershire

Set by Words & Graphics Ltd.
Anstey, Leicestershire
Printed and bound in Great Britain by
T. J. International Ltd., Padstow, Cornwall

This book is printed on acid-free paper

1

'I would have saved him. There must have been a way, and I would have found it!' John Haversley insisted.

His enthusiasm heightened the colour in his face, and the sunlight gleamed on his fair hair. Anne March smiled her approval of the familiar claim dutifully, noticing how his strong feelings made his eyes sparkle.

Peter Staunton shrugged his broad shoulders.

'So you say. But there are others who were with him in his last day, and they claim he did not wish to be rescued, that he preferred to die a martyr's death for the sake of his son.'

It was an old debate and Anne had lost count of the number of times she had listened to it, ever since Charles the First, King of England, had died at Whitehall over seven years earlier. Since

1

then his judges and executioners, Parliament, had ruled England, though everybody knew that the real power was held by Oliver Cromwell, the Lord Protector, the general who had defeated Charles, sent him to the scaffold, and now dominated his kingdom.

John Haversley was frowning now, his long fingers fretting the narrow border of lace on his white linen collar, and Anne knew that it was time to intervene before he grew angry.

'Don't let us talk about the past. We can't change it.'

John bowed stiffly.

'As you wish, Anne. What would you rather talk about? The prospects for the crops? How many lambs survived the late snow?'

Peter Staunton laughed softly.

'You know I'd be glad to talk about such matters all day, but I'm afraid that would bore Anne even more.'

She stood up, obliging them to rise politely as well.

'Let us go and look at my roses. The

blossoms were out early this year.'

Obediently the two young men escorted Anne from the secluded corner of the garden where they had been enjoying the late spring sunshine and obediently admired the fragrant rose bushes, ignoring the fact that around them the weeds flourished and the hedges were running wild.

For a few minutes Anne was able to pretend that life was as it should have been, that she was a lady of leisure with two eligible but very different young men dancing attendance on her. John was barely two inches taller than she was, but he was graceful and elegantly dressed. Even though his clothes were a sober grey they were of fine cloth and his hair almost reached his shoulders. In contrast Peter Staunton was a big man, his cheerful face attractive rather than handsome, and his hair was cut short. His clothes were plain and hardwearing, suitable for his constant work on the land. Anne remembered that time was passing and that she still had much to do in the house, and was wondering how to hint to the young men that it was time they left when Peter Staunton gazed down the drive.

'Someone is coming, Anne; and I don't think it is your father.'

Soon she could see the rider well enough to realise that he was indeed a stranger. Unknown riders often signified trouble nowadays and when he reached them Anne was standing ready to greet him but with Peter and John close behind her, ready to help if that proved necessary. Anne appeared calm but inwardly she was relieved to see that the rider was dressed in serviceable travelling clothes, not in the uniform of a Parliamentary soldier, so the visit was not likely to be official.

The horseman greeted them with a cheerful grin. 'Is the master of the house, Sir Edward March, about?' he asked.

'He is. I am his daughter,' Anne said coolly.

'You'll do.'

Without even dismounting, he took a white document from inside his coat and bent down to hand it to her.

'What is this about?' she demanded, reluctant to take it.

'Just give it to your father,' the man said easily, gathering up his reins. Anne realised that he was about to turn and ride away.

'Stop! My father may have to give you a reply!'

He shook his head. 'I was told to deliver the letter, and that was all. Goodbye, mistress!'

She stood helplessly watching him as he spurred his horse back down the drive, and then looked at the letter. It was addressed boldly to Sir Edward March, but she did not recognise the seal stamped in the red wax.

'It must be from one of my father's friends,' she said finally. Her father rarely left home nowadays, but kept up a correspondence with acquaintances he had known in better times.

Peter was looking at the sun as it

started its decline in the west. 'It's time I got back,' he commented. 'Are you coming, John?'

'Yes. My mother will be expecting me.'

They strolled towards March House, the rosy bricks of the stately Jacobean mansion glowing in the sunlight, and made their way to the stable yard where John's horse was waiting to carry him back to Haversley Manor. At twenty-three he was nominally head of the comfortable estate surrounding the Manor; but his widowed mother had run it efficiently since her husband had died eighteen years before and showed no signs of preparing to surrender control to her son, who was quite content to enjoy his comfortable income without doing too much to earn it.

In a way, his father's death had come at an opportune time, shortly before the outbreak of hostilities between King and Parliament. Throughout the war, Mistress Haversley had skilfully given whichever side appeared to be winning to understand that her husband would certainly have supported them if he had survived, and so had managed to keep the estate intact and prosperous while many of her neighbours had suffered for their obvious allegiances. When they reproached her for her deviousness she simply told them she was doing it to protect her son.

There was the sound of hooves behind them as they reached the stable yard and they turned to see a showy chestnut approaching them. John gave an exclamation of pleasure and went to greet its rider.

'Sir Edward! That's a fine new horse you have acquired!'

Sir Edward March smiled and leant down to shake John's hand. 'I've had him nearly a week now, and I'm very satisfied with him.'

Looking round, he saw Peter Staunton standing by Anne, and his smile faded as he gave a curt nod.

'Staunton!'

'Sir Edward!'

Peter's bow was ignored as Sir Edward and John began an animated conversation about the chestnut, and the big man turned to Anne.

'I must go now. You know I like to be there for the evening milking.'

She walked with him for a few yards, biting her lip with embarrassment at her father's rudeness.

'I'm sorry,' she began, but Peter shook his head, smiling.

'I'm well used to Sir Edward and his opinion of me,' he said comfortably. He glanced round, and then said in a low tone, 'I gave old Joseph six bottles of wine. Make sure Sir Edward gets his fair share.'

He sketched a quick farewell bow to her. She watched him go regretfully as he began to stride out towards his home, Staunton Grange. She enjoyed his company and thought it unreasonable that Sir Edward should treat a man with a good house and estate and a comfortable fortune as if he were an inferior. Sir Edward, however, was very firm in his opinion.

Peter's father had been a gentleman, but Sir Edward had been horrified to discover that the French woman his neighbour had unexpectedly brought home as a bride was a commoner with not the slightest trace of blue or even gentle blood.

'His grandfather is a farmer and in trade!' he often said scornfully to Anne, who had given up trying to point out that Peter's grandfather in fact owned vineyards which produced superb wines that people considered it a privilege to be allowed to buy.

A worse fault than his wife's low birth, though Anne did not discuss this with her father, had been Master Staunton's ambivalent support for the Royalist cause. In the uneasy days before fighting began, when people were choosing sides, he had sometimes pointed out Charles' faults as a king and had even been heard to say that His Majesty had to bear some of the responsibility for the approaching Civil War.

Shortly before hostilities began in 1642 he had left his steward in charge of his estates and taken his wife and young son to his father-in-law's vineyards, intending to stay there for the few months that the conflict was expected to last. Both he and his wife had died of a fever a year later, leaving Peter Staunton to be reared in France by his grandfather, and Peter had finally returned to England in 1652, only to find his lands neglected and his steward treating the house as his own.

He had promptly expelled the steward and begun to restore the land himself using the knowledge of cultivation which he had learned in France until his estate was flourishing and productive. Now he divided his time between England and France.

John Haversley mounted his waiting horse and took his leave of Anne with a flourish of his wide-brimmed hat.

'That's a fine lad who can appreciate

horseflesh,' Sir Edward commented. Anne smiled but did not reply, her eyes watching Joseph, her manservant, lead Sir Edward's chestnut into its stable. She had been surprised by its acquisition and had even dared to question whether they could afford it, only to have her quibbles indignantly dismissed by Sir Edward.

'A gentleman must have a horse worthy of his station!' he had declared. 'Are you suggesting that I cannot manage our finances competently?'

In fact this was exactly what she had been hinting, though she dared not say so openly, so she had bowed her head and let Sir Edward reprove her.

Now she handed her father the letter. 'A messenger brought this a few minutes ago, but would not wait for an answer.'

Sir Edward stuffed the document into his pocket and went into the house to change his riding coat. Anne made her way to the kitchen, not to give orders but to begin to prepare the vegetables for the evening meal. Martha, Joseph's wife, was busy making pastry. There was a familiar smell.

'Rabbit stew?' Anne questioned, and Martha nodded vigorously.

'The master likes my rabbit stew,' she said firmly. This was just as well, thought Anne, for it appeared very frequently for dinner.

Soon afterwards Joseph himself came into the kitchen and drew a mug of ale.

'Master Staunton told me he brought some wine,' Anne remarked.

'That he did — four bottles,' Joseph returned, and stared into her eyes, daring her to contradict him and knowing she would not challenge his lie.

She would have loved to do so and to denounce his veiled insolence, but that was impossible because she could not risk the couple taking offence and leaving.

Sir Edward had inherited a prosperous estate and a fair-sized fortune, most of which he had given to the cause of

King Charles in the expectation of being suitably rewarded when the king's opponents were crushed. Instead, after the king's defeat and execution he had been fined as a malignant and forced to sell much of his estate.

He had formerly employed a steward who had run his estates efficiently but he could not afford that luxury now. Convinced that a gentleman should not behave like a farmer, he had made no attempt to learn how to administer his estate properly himself, so his land and house suffered from his ignorance and neglect, reducing his income even further. Servants had grown tired of waiting to be paid and had gradually drifted away until the staff which had once maintained the big house had been reduced to Joseph and Martha.

Privately Anne considered that the middle-aged couple were very fortunate. They had the run of the house and the estate as well as a rent-free cottage. Once Joseph might have been hauled before the magistrate for poaching, but now the rabbits, hares and pheasants he caught were the mainstay of their diet, together with the chickens and pigs he raised.

Anne suspected that while she and her father dined on an inordinate amount of rabbit stew and the occasional rabbit pie, it was possible that Joseph and Martha were enjoying more roast chicken and pheasants than their master.

When the vegetables were prepared Anne went to inspect the dining-room. Beneath the elaborate plaster ceiling the great oak table, which could easily have seated twenty, dominated the room. Quickly Anne set the table with the pewter plates and cutlery which she and her father would require. Once the table would have glittered with plate and crystal, but the family silver had disappeared during one financial crisis and her father had informed her that pewter would be more practical.

'Martha hasn't got the time to spend polishing silver,' he had said.

Martha did not seem to have the time to do much beyond cook their simple meals and do a bit of laundry. Most of the rooms of the great house were now shut up and disused, but it was Anne who ensured that the few that she and her father used regularly were clean and tidy.

She laid linen napkins by the plates, folding them so that the holes and frayed edges were concealed, then went to her room and prepared for dinner. This meant changing into one of her two good dresses. Looking at her reflection to check her appearance gave her no great pleasure. She had no maid to curl her hair fashionably, and although the pale oval of her face was dominated by her dark eyes, she was not considered pretty. Her father had once said that she had the kind of looks that improved with age, a remark which had not cheered her.

She went down to check that dinner was nearly ready, but her father's voice summoned her into the library. His colour was high and he was staring at the open letter in front of him.

'This letter is from Hawkins, my lawyer in London, and he and his wife wish to keep their daughter safe by sending her to stay here.'

Anne's eyes widened. She knew what a low opinion her father had of lawyers and was sure he would never accept the girl as a guest.

'You must write to him at once and tell him his request is not possible! How foolish of him to dare suggest it!'

Her father looked at the letter again. 'He is not asking if she may come. He is saying that she will come.'

'Then when she arrives we must find suitable lodgings for her elsewhere. She could stay with some respectable widow in the village. She can't expect to stay here.'

But her father was shaking his head slowly. 'No, Anne. She will stay here.' He avoided meeting her eyes. 'Her father has done me several favours. I cannot turn his daughter away. Tell

Martha to get a room ready for her tomorrow.'

'Are you sure?'

He looked at her bleakly. 'I do not expect you to question what I say.'

There could be no more discussion, but lying awake that night Anne fretted angrily. She would have to prepare the room, not Martha, and she would have to look after the girl when she came. The poor girl would be tired and home-sick, unused to the ways of the country, and it was understandable after all that Lawyer Hawkins should try to protect his dear daughter from the dreaded plague. Eagerness to get her away from the city must have overridden all other considerations.

The next morning Martha was very interested to hear the news that there was to be a guest in the house.

'A lady from London? Will she be very grand?'

'She's just a girl, Martha.'

'Will she bring a maid with her?'

This was a new idea. Would the

17

cherished daughter have been sent off by herself? Perhaps some reliable maidservant would accompany her. To be on the safe side, Anne swept and dusted two rooms.

Nobody appeared the next day. At six o'clock precisely Sir Edward and Anne took their places at the dining-table. Once again the main dish was rabbit stew. When Joseph filled Sir Edward's glass with wine he tasted it, and smiled with pleasure. It was obviously superior to the vinegary stuff which was all he could usually afford.

'Peter Staunton brought you a present of some wine yesterday,' Anne said quietly.

Sir Edward enjoyed another mouthful before he replied, rather coldly, 'I suppose he has just come back from another trip to see his low relatives in France and is trying to ingratiate himself with us, Anne. I was not pleased to see you treating John Haversley and Master Staunton as equals yesterday. The man is nothing but a common farmer, and you must remember that we have noble connections.'

Sir Edward claimed to be a very distant cousin of an earl who seemed to be unaware of his relatives' existence, but Sir Edward still cherished the belief that there was a blood link between them.

'Master Staunton is one of my few friends, Father.'

'You have John Haversley for company. He may not be pleased to see you being so pleasant to another man.'

'John Haversley has no right to judge my choice of friends.'

'He will have eventually. You know what I mean.'

Anne knew that Sir Edward had assumed for some years that she and John would eventually marry, though he had said little about it and had certainly never mentioned it to John's mother, who might have other ideas for her darling son. Mistress Haversley would want more than vague 'noble connections' as a dowry, Anne thought wistfully. John was handsome but he seemed to regard her as a friend to whom he could pour out the details of the deeds he would have accomplished for King Charles if only he had been born earlier.

The meal proceeded in silence while Anne brooded on her future. She was already twenty, old for marriage. She could not think of any way she might somehow meet someone who would care for her and whom her father would consider eligible. Was she doomed to follow this dull routine for decades, looking after the house and her father, fading into an elderly spinster, unless some disaster disrupted her life? At least the Hawkins girl might provide some distraction.

2

Anne was up early as usual the next morning and soon hard at work. Whatever her father thought of Peter Staunton working like a farmer, Sir Edward did nothing to stop his daughter working like a farmer's wife. There was butter to be churned and stocks of preserves and pickles to be checked. Martha had brought a basket of eggs.

'Do you want them boiled or do you want omelettes?' she asked.

Anne counted the eggs. 'We could have some boiled, and I could make some custard with the rest,' she decided.

'Fancy stuff!' Martha said disapprovingly.

'My father likes them, and they are good for his digestion,' Anne said firmly, knowing this would silence

Martha. She and her husband might take advantage of their position, and Joseph might steal Sir Edward's wine and Martha do no more work than she had to, but both of them were devoted to their master.

It was soon after their light mid-day meal, and Anne had returned to the kitchen when Martha came scurrying to find her, her eyes bright with excitement.

'Joseph says there's a carriage turning into the drive!'

With only a minute to transform herself from cook to lady of the house, hastily Anne undid the strings of the apron protecting her dress.

'My father is in the library,' she snapped. 'Tell him we have a visitor!'

Was it one of Sir Edward's friends breaking a journey to call on his old acquaintance, or some official of the Commonwealth bringing yet more trouble?

Sir Edward and Anne met on the steps of the house. If the visitor should be unwelcome it would be easier to discourage them by not admitting them to the house itself. They watched the carriage approach and draw up. It was modern and elegant, drawn by two good horses, and the coachman gave Anne a cheeky smile before doffing his hat in salute to her father, and then he leapt down and went to open the carriage door and hold out his hand to assist the occupant of the carriage to alight. Anne stared and heard Martha, peering round the door, give a startled gasp.

The Puritan domination of the country meant that virtually all women wore grey or black. Any bright colour was considered to indicate an unacceptably frivolous nature or even moral faults, but the petite figure of the girl emerging from the carriage was swathed in an extravagant blue velvet cloak that Anne coveted on sight.

The visitor pushed back her hood, revealing golden ringlets, and as Anne and her father came slowly down the steps to greet her, she smiled brilliantly, bobbed a token curtsey, and did not bother to wait for Sir Edward to address her first.

'Sir Edward! And you must be Anne. I told my father he should have given you more warning but he was desperate to get me away from London as soon as possible. I am Lucy Hawkins.'

Lucy had large brown eyes and her smiling mouth had full lips. Her nose was small and slightly tilted. It was definitely not an aristocratic face, but it was extremely pretty. As she moved towards them Anne could see a blue silk dress with a lace collar under the cloak, which was held at the throat by a large gold brooch.

In spite of her words, the girl showed no embarrassment at having arrived to stay so unexpectedly nor any awareness that she was speaking to her social superiors.

Behind her a middle-aged woman dressed simply in grey had also descended from the carriage and was watching critically. Lucy indicated her casually.

'My maid, Bella. If you will tell her where my room is, she and Thomas will take my baggage up.'

'I'll show her,' Martha said firmly, popping out of the doorway. Meanwhile Sir Edward and Anne, rather than welcoming their guest to their home, had to hurry to keep up with her as she swept up the steps and into the house. She inspected the entrance hall with undisguised interest.

'How quaint!' she pronounced. 'My father said that people in the country preferred to keep to the old fashions.'

Anne closed her eyes and waited for a furious explosion from her father, but when it did not come she opened them cautiously and saw that Sir Edward was eyeing Lucy Hawkins with baffled bewilderment.

'Your man, Thomas, can drive the carriage round to the stable and unharness the horses when he has delivered your luggage,' Anne said hurriedly, trying to reassert the Marches' authority, but Lucy shook her head.

'Thomas isn't staying. He would appreciate some ale, I'm sure, but then he is to start back with the coach immediately.'

Sir Edward recovered the initiative sufficiently to usher the newcomer into the drawing room, where Joseph soon appeared with a tray of glasses and a bottle of Peter Staunton's wine.

'I will take you to your room,' Anne stated when this refreshment was finished, and she led her up the broad staircase to the room which had been made ready, where they found Martha helping Lucy's maid to unpack her pile of luggage while taking every opportunity to examine each garment as it emerged. The bedchamber was a large one, filled with sunlight and with a pleasant view over the grounds. Lucy inspected everything with apparent pleasure.

'What a lovely room!' She examined the bed and the furniture and then turned to Anne. 'I shall like it here! But could I have another coverlet? The country seems colder than the city, but I won't need a fire lit till the evening. And perhaps some dried sweet herbs in the closets? They do smell a little musty, as if they haven't been used for some time. The sun is beautiful, but I do hope the curtains are thick enough to keep out the light. If not, I am sure you can do something about them.'

Her brilliant smile made it clear that she took it for granted that her requests would be satisfied. Lucy Hawkins was clearly used to getting things exactly as she wanted them, and Martha was soon scurrying around to correct the deficiencies, eager to please the lady from London.

In less than an hour the whole balance of life at March Hall seemed to have shifted. When Anne had risen that morning, all activity had been centred on serving and pleasing Sir Edward, but now it was Lucy Hawkins who had to be satisfied. After hurriedly instructing

Martha to show Bella her room when there was an opportunity and to bring some food for Lucy and her maid, Anne sought out Sir Edward and found him sitting in the library.

'Father,' she began, 'what are we to do with Miss Hawkins?'

He looked at her with alarm. 'What is the matter? Is she being difficult?'

'Well, no. But you must agree that she is very different from what we expected.'

He nodded, and then fidgeted uneasily. 'I admit I did not expect anyone so charming. She will be good company for you, Anne.'

In other words, Lucy Hawkins was Anne's responsibility. Fuming, Anne made for the kitchen where she found Martha busy chopping and kneading.

'Miss Hawkins is obviously accustomed to the best,' the woman explained. 'I think I'd better prepare some more little dishes for dinner.'

'I suppose what we normally eat isn't good enough for her,' Anne remarked sarcastically, and was quietly furious when Martha nodded agreement. She hurried back up the stairs, determined to make the difference between Sir Edward March's daughter and a lawyer's daughter quite clear to Miss Hawkins, but was disarmed by the visitor's welcoming smile.

'I trust you had a good journey?' Anne enquired as coldly as she could, but Lucy responded cheerfully.

'Yes, indeed! We had to spend two nights at inns, but of course I had a sitting room as well as a bedchamber so it was quite comfortable. I enjoyed driving through the countryside as well, because I have rarely left London before. My father is always too busy to leave his affairs, and this is the first time he has thought me old enough to travel on my own.'

'You do look very young to undertake such a journey.'

'I was seventeen five months ago, and anyway I had Thomas and Bella to look after me.'

Before any more could be said there was a discreet tap on the door. It was Thomas, the coachman and messenger, come to say goodbye to his mistress. Lucy Hawkins instructed him to tell her father that she had arrived safely, and soon afterwards they heard the carriage driving away.

'Is your maid satisfied with her room?'

'I think so. Bella hasn't complained, anyway. Is she near your maid?'

Anne gritted her teeth. 'I don't have a maid. Martha helps with the housework and cooking.' Lucy's expression of scarcely-hidden pity made her carry on. 'We lead a very quiet, simple life here.'

'Of course,' Lucy said, her voice oozing tactful sympathy.

'Would you like to look round the gardens before the light fades?' Anne asked, confident at least her garden must be larger than any Lucy had in London. She led the way down the main stairs and out into the sunlit grounds. Lucy exclaimed with genuine delight at the sight of Anne's beloved roses, and after Anne had demonstrated her superior horticultural knowledge for half-an-hour she felt more charitable towards her guest.

'I hope you will not feel too homesick,' she remarked. 'This place is very different from London. Still, I expect your father was very pleased to get you away from the plague. Is it very bad?'

Lucy did not answer. Instead, to Anne's surprise, she seemed to be suppressing a laugh.

'Is anything wrong?' she said sharply. 'The threat of plague is not a laughing matter.'

'No, of course not,' Lucy said hastily, but then giggled openly. 'It is just that my father was not completely frank with you, Anne. Of course there have been some cases of plague, but there always are at this time of the year. The truth is, my father was not really concerned about the plague. He wanted to get me away from Matthew!'

'Matthew?'

'Matthew Cox.' Lucy's eyes grew soft and dreamy. 'He is nineteen, and very, very handsome, but he is only a clerk in a merchant's warehouse, so of course my father disapproved of our acquaintanceship.'

Suddenly everything became clear to Anne. This was a story of high romance, the kind she had read about in her father's collections of plays and ballads. Lawyer Hawkins had sent his daughter into the country to separate two young lovers! Her heart filled with sympathy.

'You poor thing! Are you very unhappy? At least you can write to Matthew from here.'

Lucy showed no sign of a broken heart. Instead she shrugged and giggled again. 'I enjoyed flirting with Matthew, but he was getting too serious. He even began to talk of marriage! As if I would marry a clerk!' She shook her head firmly. 'Coming here away from him suits me very well, though of course I didn't let Father know that. I expect Matthew will soon go looking for another wealthy sweetheart, and I can see if I like life in the country.'

Her romantic fantasies destroyed, Anne considered the implications of what Lucy had said.

'Is there any chance of you moving to the country?'

The young girl shrugged again. 'The war has impoverished many of the King's followers. My dowry would be enough to persuade plenty of well-born gentlemen with land but no money to overlook my lack of blue blood. I might even marry someone with a title.'

'You aim high,' Anne said coolly.

'England is changing. We no longer have a king, so we no longer have a court, and half the noblemen of England are starving in France with Charles Stuart. Many of them would be glad to find an heiress, no matter how lowly her birth, and my father is a man of standing and respect. I don't want to spend the rest of my life in a lawyer's house in London.'

'Still, you are only seventeen.'

Lucy laughed. 'True. I can spend the next few years being courted by any number of eligible young men before I finally make my choice. It will be fun.'

Anne was silent. Lucy might be only seventeen, but she was obviously far more worldly-wise and experienced than her hostess.

They went back to the house to prepare for dinner, Anne having warned Lucy that they kept country hours and dined early. She had also murmured that they believed in simple fare, and Lucy might find their meal very plain by London standards.

She need not have bothered. That night there was roast chicken as well as rabbit pie and a range of vegetable dishes. Lucy might not have realised what an effort Martha had made on her behalf, but she displayed a healthy young appetite.

The next morning Anne came downstairs to discover that Sir Edward had ridden over to the nearest town early that morning, leaving word that he would not be back till evening. Anne suspected that this unexpected absence was his way of avoiding any problems that might arise with Lucy.

Martha was at work in the kitchen earlier than usual. She was full of questions about the visitors, and was obviously pleased to hear that her cooking had been appreciated. Anne realised a little wryly that she had not been the only one to find their day to day life a trifle drab and boring and that Martha was enjoying the break in routine. Bella appeared eventually, explained that her mistress always breakfasted in bed, and took her up a tray. In fact Anne had time to get through quite a number of her domestic tasks before Lucy finally appeared, dressed in apple-green and ready to be entertained.

Meanwhile Anne had decided that the visitor had a duty to accommodate herself to life at the Hall.

'Good morning,' she greeted Lucy. 'Martha will find you an apron to protect your dress and then you can help me with the dusting.'

Lucy looked gently amused at the suggestion that she should help with the housekeeping.

'I don't do such tasks. We have servants to do them.'

'You are fortunate,' Anne said curtly. 'Here I do them.'

'But I do not,' Lucy said with polite finality.

She agreed to help Anne take some scraps to the farmyard, only to retreat rapidly when she found it involved mud and disagreeable smells. Exasperated, Anne confronted her.

'Lucy Hawkins, you should have stayed at home if you want the comforts of a house with plenty of servants to do your bidding. Here we have Joseph and Martha, and me. How do you spend your days in London?'

'I visit my friends. We buy things.'

'Your friends are a long way away and

there no merchants near here. What are you going to do to pass the time while you are here if you won't help me?'

Lucy thought for a while, and then her face brightened. 'I can sew!'

'We do not need anything embroidered.'

'I can mend and darn as well. I like sewing.'

Anne relaxed.

'In that case I can find you plenty to do here. I hate sewing. After lunch we must go through the linen store.'

They did this, finding enough work to keep Lucy busy for days and in fact Lucy was busy darning some linen towels and Anne was frowning over some housekeeping lists when there was the tramp of boots along the corridor and John Haversley knocked briefly at the morning-room door and entered without waiting for a response.

'Anne, I'm on my way to see Peter Staunton, but Mother asked me to return this book,' he began, and then realised that as well as Anne the room held a very pretty young girl with her blonde head bent modestly over her work. The two girls rose in a flurry of skirts, and Anne introduced the newcomer.

'This is Master John Haversley, Lucy. He is a neighbour of ours. John, Lucy Hawkins has come to visit us all the way from London.'

John scarcely spared Anne a glance. His eyes were fixed on Lucy, who blushed as he stared at her.

'I trust you will be staying for some time,' he said gallantly.

'That depends on what happens in London,' Anne said firmly. 'Have you come to see Father?'

He turned towards her for the first time. 'Only to return this book.'

'Then if you give it to me we will not detain you from your meeting.'

He produced a small volume and gave it to Anne, his attention still fixed on Lucy.

'I trust we will meet again,' he told her. 'Will you be at church on Sunday?'

'Of course,' Lucy responded, and Anne watched them smile at each other.

Once he had gone Lucy was full of questions which Anne answered briefly and reluctantly, but the younger girl looked satisfied with what she learned.

'So he has a good estate and no brothers or sisters to maintain.'

'He has his mother, who guards him jealously.'

A secret, smug smile tugged momentarily at Lucy's lips.

'Mothers like me. I'm pretty, young and rich. They think they will be able to manage me.'

She looked up at Anne with sudden alarm.

'But do you care for him? Do you want to marry him?'

Anne shook her head and forced herself to laugh. 'Me? No! We are friends, like brother and sister, that is all.'

Lucy fell silent, but there was a gleam in her eye.

3

Anne reproached herself for the way she had handled the situation. 'I might as well have pushed John out of the door,' she told herself guiltily. 'And Lucy is little more than a child. Of course she was curious about a good-looking young gentleman, especially when there is so little to interest her round here.'

At least the rest of the day had gone smoothly enough. Sir Edward had reappeared in time for dinner and had treated Lucy with heavy politeness during the meal. Much to her surprise, Anne had not had to prepare or cook any of it. When she had gone down to the kitchen she had found Bella there, busy helping Martha. Anne's offer of assistance had quickly been rejected.

'Bella and I can manage perfectly well,' Martha had told her firmly.

Anne had gone back to Lucy, not sure how she would receive the news that her personal maid was acting as the cook's assistant, but Lucy had nodded placidly.

'They'll be having a good gossip. Bella used to be maid to a lady at a big house in the country until the war ruined the family, and she has never really liked working in the city, while I expect your Martha will want to hear all about London.'

It soon became clear that the two servants had indeed struck up a warm friendship. Bella was quite ready to help in the kitchen while she gossiped with Martha, and Anne found that she herself had become positively unwelcome there. Freed from cooking, she could complete her household chores far more quickly. When Lucy was tired of sewing she decided that a little light work in the garden was an acceptable activity and under Anne's instructions she industriously deadheaded roses and watered plants.

On Sunday they went to church. Anne found this a weekly ordeal since the benign pastor who had tended the parish for nearly forty years had been summarily dismissed and replaced by a Presbyterian minister whose hour-long sermons tended to concentrate on the death and damnation that awaited anyone who disagreed with his strict principles or the rule of Thomas Cromwell, Lord Protector, and his most blistering attacks always seemed to be aimed directly at Sir Edward March, who listened stony-faced, but never deigned to show any reaction.

Lucy, following Anne's anxious advice, wore a demure silver-grey dress and cloak, though the lace at her neck was generously applied and of the finest quality. The small party from March House was the last to arrive, and several faces turned towards them as they entered.

Anne, dressed in her usual rusty black, realised that the church was much fuller than usual, and then it dawned on her that the parishioners were gazing at Lucy as she was ushered in by Sir Edward. Of course! Word would have spread rapidly about the interesting young visitor staying at March House, and everyone had come to see Lucy.

The party from March House were hidden from the view of most of the congregation during the service by their high box pew, but once it had finished and they emerged into the churchyard they found themselves being scrutinised by villagers who were lingering deliberately in order to examine Lucy and her fashionable clothes as closely as possible. Those who could claim acquaintance with Sir Edward greeted him warmly and then waited to be introduced to his charming guest. Anne waited, smiling politely at those who saluted her.

'A pack of fools, eager to see the latest novelty.'

Anne turned round, her head held proudly high, and found the speaker, Major Wolford, close behind her and looking scornfully at the group around Sir Edward. Major Wolford and his troops of Roundheads represented Cromwell's authority in the area. He always behaved with careful correctness when he encountered Sir Edward or his daughter, but she suspected that he held the surviving Royalists in some contempt, and she was a little frightened of him. Now, as he saw Anne looking at him, he bowed slightly.

'Mistress Hawkins is my friend,' she said coldly.

'Then she is fortunate. Not many well-born ladies would befriend a lawyer's daughter.'

This was what Anne had been feeling herself, of course, but she would not give him the satisfaction of agreeing with him. While she wondered what answer to make, she heard an eager voice calling her name.

'Anne! Over here!'

John Haversley was waving at her, his mother by his side, and Anne was aware of Lucy going to greet him. Gratefully

Anne abandoned Major Wolford without replying to his comment.

'If I'd known there would be so many people waiting for us I would not have come! I feel I am being stared at like some strange monster at a fair!' Anne complained to John.

He laughed. 'Don't worry. Everybody has come to see Lucy, not you. Doesn't she look beautiful?'

Unaware how tactless she might find these remarks, he hurried forward to negotiate the introduction of his mother and Lucy, then Sir Edward engaged him in conversation, and Anne found herself temporarily ignored again.

'So this is your guest,' said a quiet voice. 'The villagers have been talking of nothing else all week.'

This time Anne turned round with an exclamation of pleasure. Peter Staunton was speaking to her, but his eyes were fixed on Lucy and Mistress Haversley.

'I am glad we have given them some amusement,' Anne said. 'What do you think of her?'

Peter Staunton pursed his lips. 'She is very young and very pretty,' he commented. 'Her dress indicates wealth and taste, and Mistress Haversley appears to be finding her very charming.'

Anne watched Mistress Haversley laughing at something Lucy had said, then saw John Haversley and her father join in the laughter. They seemed to have forgotten about her and she felt isolated, ignored by those in the happy circle. Lucy had stolen her friends. Suddenly she felt the recent discontent and uncertainties well up.

'She is pretty,' Anne heard herself say, 'and it appears that her father is wealthy. Unfortunately she is also of low birth, which must override any other qualities.'

As soon as she had spoken the words she was appalled. Why had she said that, and to Peter Staunton, of all people? She, who knew how much he had endured from people who thought themselves his betters! Anne took a step towards him hurriedly.

'Peter, I didn't mean that!'

He looked at her without expression, bowed, then turned and walked deliberately away without another word. She would have followed him but at that moment John came to her side, eager to tell her of arrangements that had been made for the two girls to visit his mother the following day, and she was forced to listen, to say the right things, while wondering frantically what she could do to atone for her tactless words to Peter Staunton.

Soon Sir Edward excused himself from the people who still clustered round him and he and the two girls began to walk back to March House. He was smiling contentedly.

'Our villagers are a pleasant group,' he commented to Lucy. 'Of course, the courtesy and friendship they showed you reflects the esteem they feel for me.'

Lucy gave him a brilliant smile. 'I am so happy to be here with you!'

Neither of them noticed how quiet Anne was on the way home, nor how she hardly said a word for the rest of the day. She kept trying to convince herself that Peter would realise that she had not meant those foolish words. Surely they had known each other long enough for him to give her the benefit of the doubt? Most probably he would ride over some day during the next week and she would have the opportunity to apologise to him.

But the days passed and he did not appear. John Haversley called twice, once to escort them to Haversley Manor, where his mother welcomed them warmly and seemed very taken with Lucy.

'A very well-mannered girl,' she murmured to Anne, 'and I gather her father is wealthy?'

'I believe so.'

'And she is his only child?'

'Yes.'

Mistress Haversley said no more on the subject, but her attentions to Lucy grew even more marked.

Anne prepared for church the following Sunday with great care, but Peter Staunton was nowhere to be seen.

'Has Master Staunton gone to France?' she asked one of his tenants, but was told that the master did not plan to leave for some weeks yet.

Convinced that he was deliberately avoiding her, Anne decided to take matters into her own hands, and the following day she asked Joseph to saddle the horse which she rode when she was not wanted for farm work and rode over to Staunton Grange, informing her father and Lucy that she wanted to consult Peter about some hens which did not seem to be laying as many eggs as usual.

Anne rode slowly, rehearsing her apology, but was aware of the unkempt, neglected look of her father's land compared to the tidy, fruitful fields surrounding Staunton Grange. The house itself was comparatively small, and the Stauntons had not remodelled the rosy Tudor brick building but had cherished it carefully. The mullioned windows shone and everything was in good repair, as it was in the farmyard where she found Peter Staunton in his shirt sleeves helping some of his workers to store hay in the great barn.

She reined in her horse and watched him, trying to imagine her father labouring alongside his tenants, till Peter raised his head and saw her. She waved eagerly but he merely nodded politely to acknowledge her presence before he spoke briefly to those who were helping him and then walked slowly towards her.

'Mistress March,' was his unsmiling greeting.

'Peter . . . I must talk to you. In private.'

He went to speak, then hesitated, as if biting back the words he had been going to use. 'Are you sure we have anything to say to each other?' he said finally.

'Yes!' she insisted. 'Please, listen to me!'

His lips tightened, and then he held out a hand to help her dismount before he beckoned a labourer and gave the horse to his charge before leading her into the house. The furniture in the room they entered was old, the heavily carved oak black with age, but it had been lovingly polished, and the room was clean, warm and welcoming.

Anne remained standing, even when Peter politely offered her a chair, and he waited silently for what she had to say.

'Peter,' she began, having mentally rehearsed the words dozens of times during the previous week, 'I thought we had known each other well enough and long enough for you to realise that I did not mean what I said after church that day.'

Again there was a pause before his reply. 'I thought I did,' he said heavily. 'I thought we were friends and that you saw me as an equal. Then, after that incident, I decided that what I had mistaken for friendship had probably been just good manners, and that you had said what you really felt. After all, you are Sir Edward March's daughter.'

'We are friends, and I didn't mean what I said!'

'Then why did you say it?' he demanded angrily.

She closed her eyes, near to tears. 'I was jealous.'

His voice was carefully flat. 'You were jealous? Because of the attention John Haversley was paying to Lucy Hawkins? Do you really care for him so much? I don't think you need worry. She is just a novelty, a pretty distraction.'

Her eyes flew open indignantly. 'I wasn't jealous of what John might feel for Lucy!'

His silence forced her to continue, and suddenly all the feelings she had been suppressing for a long time welled up in her.

'I admit I was jealous because everybody was paying attention to her and I was feeling lonely and deserted, but that wasn't all. I was jealous of her because she is young and pretty, because her father is wealthy and she has pretty clothes, while I spend my days growing older in a decaying house, wondering what will become of me when my father dies and the money has all gone.' The tears were running down her face now. 'I am jealous of her because she sees the future as something to welcome and enjoy, knowing that she can choose what she wants to do, while I am scared and helpless.'

Sobs prevented her saying more, but Peter's arm was round her as he supported her to a chair and he had a handkerchief ready when she sank down gratefully. She was aware of his leaving the room, and then she abandoned herself to her tears, weeping until she was exhausted.

At last she heaved a deep sigh and wiped her eyes, painfully aware that she had made a complete fool of herself, and she desperately wondered how she could escape from the situation. A minute later the door opened and Peter came in carrying a tray which he set down carefully.

'There is mulled wine,' he said calmly. 'My housekeeper recommends it as a soothing and healthy drink. However, I have added brandy in case you feel the need for something stronger.'

Anne laughed with a touch of hysteria. 'The mulled wine, please.'

She drank the warm, spicy drink he handed her slowly. Only when she had emptied the glass did she raise her head and look directly at Peter.

'I'm sorry.'

'For what? For what you said after church or for creating a scene now which had — admit it — embarrassed us both?'

This time her laughter was genuine. 'For both.'

'Then I accept your apology — for both.'

He refilled their glasses and pulled a chair up near hers. 'I must apologise too. I was oversensitive. I was so sure I knew you that I was shocked at what you said and didn't try to look for the reasons why you said it. You always seem to calm and in control.'

She sipped the wine reflectively. 'So you thought I was jealous of Lucy because of John?'

'Well, I know your father had always expected the two of you to marry. I thought perhaps you did too.'

She shook her head. 'I like John, and if he cared for me it would be a convenient solution to my problems. But when I saw how attracted he was by Lucy I realised that I did not love him because I wasn't jealous, and I have no wish to marry a man who obviously thinks of me as a sister and nothing more. Besides, Mistress Haversley wants a better match for her son.'

'So the real reason for your spiteful remark was your fear of the future?'

Anne sighed. 'Yes. I am scared. I am used to being Mistress Anne March of March House. But I don't even have any relatives who will take me in out of pity when my father dies. How can I survive or earn my living?'

'Are you sure the outlook is as bleak as you suggest? Your father will not leave you penniless, will he? You will have March House and the land belonging to it.'

'I hope so, but I can't even be sure of that, because my father does not confide in me. I suspect that the land, perhaps even the house itself, has been pledged in return for loans. I know that we have very little ready money, because I am the one who has to deal with the trades people, persuading them that their bills will be paid, doling out a little cash to each of them when it becomes available so that they will continue to supply us with what we need.'

She wondered whether she should tell Peter this, whether she was betraying her father's confidence, but it didn't matter. It was such a relief to tell someone else about the worries which had gnawed at her for so long.

Peter Staunton stood up and smiled down at her. 'I won't offer you any more wine, because you have got to ride home. What I can do is tell you that your fears are groundless. Even if your father dies deep in debt, do you think your friends would allow you to suffer? Stop brooding, Mistress March of March House!'

She was comforted by his words, and by the fact that they were friends again.

Peter stood by her horse as she prepared to ride home.

'There is one thing which puzzles me,' he said quietly. 'Why has your father accepted Lucy, a lawyer's daughter, as his guest? Why is he so eager to please her?'

'I have wondered. I don't know.'

4

The next few weeks were the happiest Anne could remember. There were carefree gatherings in the sun-filled gardens. John Haversley was the most frequent caller at March House. He was showing all the symptoms of boyish first love for Lucy, who obviously enjoyed his attentions, but refused to reveal how she felt herself.

'I like him, of course I do,' she told Anne. 'Nobody else has written poems about me before, even if they are not very good. In fact, they're very bad,' she commented, showing Anne the young man's latest effort. 'There are one or two good lines, but I suspect he copied them from some book of poetry.'

Peter Staunton often visited the House as well, his friendship with Anne fully restored, and he laughed when she confessed how old she felt when she watched Lucy and John.

'Wait till you fall in love. You'll be just the same.'

'They are like children playing games. I can't take them seriously.'

The contrast between Sir Edward's cool treatment of Peter Staunton and his warm treatment of Lucy continued to puzzle Anne. After all, Peter's father had been a gentleman while the Hawkins seemed to have no gently born relatives whatsoever. One day she tried to broach the subject with Lucy.

'Why did your father decide to send you to March House, Lucy? He must have other acquaintances who live in the country. Why did he choose us?'

Lucy gave her a sideways, cautious glance. 'Sir Edward and my father have had various business dealings. Perhaps he felt he knew Sir Edward well enough to be sure he would welcome me. And he knew that Sir Edward had a daughter who would be a companion to me, and so you have been. I have enjoyed being with you all this time.'

Lucy and her father exchanged letters via merchants with business in London or via army officers. After a time the lawyer's letters began to suggest that it was time his daughter returned to him, but Lucy's answers always pointed out how good the pure country air was for her health compared to the polluted atmosphere of London. Anne wondered if it was John rather than the fresh air that kept her away from the pleasures of the capital.

There were other less attractive men, and she was taken aback one day when she came downstairs to find Major Wolford standing in the entrance hall and she looked round nervously, knowing how angry her father became if one of Cromwell's soldiers entered his house. She approached him coolly when he saluted her with a low bow.

'Are you waiting to see my father? Has he been told you are here?'

He shook his head. 'I believe your father is out riding. I brought a letter for Mistress Hawkins, which your servant has taken to her. I am waiting to see if she wants to send a reply.'

It would have been impolite to leave him standing there alone, so Anne lingered in the hall, hoping that Lucy's response would come soon. She would have felt duty bound to offer some refreshment to other visitors, but knew her father would never allow Cromwell's man to be treated as a guest and for once she agreed with her father. She did not want Major Wolford to feel welcome.

'I am sorry you have had to come out of your way to bring the letter,' she remarked stiffly. 'I hope it was not too inconvenient.'

'On the contrary, I welcomed the chance to visit March House. I have always admired the building.'

Anne was silent. Every other time Major Wolford had called at March House it had been for some unpleasant confrontation with her father, and after the major had left she had usually been forced to listen to a furious denunciation by Sir Edward of the Commonwealth government and all its ways. She had not been aware that Major Wolford had taken the opportunity to appraise the house, and she found herself repelled by the thought of his cold eyes studying her home.

At that moment, fortunately, Martha bustled back with the information that Lucy would not be writing to her father for a few days. Major Wolford took his leave with punctilious politeness and Anne went to find Lucy, whom she found sitting in the shade of an oak tree, studying her father's letter with a slight frown.

'Bad news?' Anne enquired.

'Not really. Only my father says again that he wants me to go home. He says he is missing me, but that probably means he wants me where he can see me so that he knows I'm not getting into mischief.'

'Don't you want to go back to your friends and all the excitements of the city?'

'Sometimes,' Lucy said slowly. She

glanced at Anne. 'But I love it here and Bella will be heartbroken when we have to leave. It's beautiful, and I like the people.'

'Particularly John Haversley?'

Lucy blushed. 'Of course I like John, just as I like you and Peter Staunton.'

'Only you like John more.'

Lucy fidgeted. 'If you mean that I love him, I'm not sure. I like him more than anyone else I have met, but I can't decide yet whether that is love or not. I don't want to leave him.'

'Perhaps if you go back to London the separation will show you how you really feel.'

'But if I do leave and then decide I love him, how will I see him again? I think he really loves me now, but suppose he forgets about me when I am gone?'

Anne patted her hand with mock impatience. 'You will both be in the same country, only three days' travel apart, and I am sure he will not forget you! If you do love each other, you will find some way to meet again.'

'Well, I'm not going back yet,' Lucy declared resolutely.

Fine words, but a fortnight later the Hawkins' carriage rolled up the drive and Anne returned from a visit to Mistress Haversley to find both Lucy and Bella in tears. Lawyer Hawkins was not prepared to wait any longer and Thomas had been sent to take the two absentee members of his household back to London.

'I don't want to go! I won't go!' Lucy protested, although she knew she had no choice.

'Your father must be aware that it will take you a couple of days at least to prepare for the journey,' Anne comforted her. 'You will have time to say goodbye to everyone. Thomas can stay in Joseph's cottage until you are ready.'

The news of Thomas's arrival and what it meant soon spread. John Haversley appeared within hours, looking very distressed, and he and Lucy took themselves off to the garden. Peter

Staunton called by chance a little later and found Anne patrolling the paths around the rose garden where Lucy and John were conferring.

'Are you playing chaperone?' he enquired, very amused.

Anne glared at him. 'What if I am? They are young and in love and about to be separated. I don't want them to do anything stupid, like eloping.'

'There is no fear of such behaviour. Lucy is far too practical for that, and if John eloped he would probably have to take his mother with him to organise it for him.'

Anne laughed in spite of herself. 'You have no romance in you!' she scolded him.

'I'm afraid not. I'm just a farmer with no time for such high-flown ideas.'

Before she could find an appropriate reply, Lucy and John emerged from the rose garden. Lucy was red-eyed and Anne suspected that John had shed tears as well. She went towards them eagerly and Lucy summoned a wan smile while Peter put a friendly arm around John's shoulders and took him away for a walk.

'You are right, of course,' Lucy said sadly. 'I will have to obey my father and go back to London, but John and I have sworn that we will see each other again.'

Bella had reluctantly started packing the next morning when Sir Edward sent Martha to tell Anne that he wished to see her in the library. She found him restless and frowning.

'I have made a decision,' he said abruptly. 'It is not safe for Lucy and her maid to make such a long journey with only the coachman to look after them. I will escort them to London. Will you please see that my luggage is got ready? Joseph will accompany me, of course.'

Anne stared at him, astonished. Her father's trips to London had been few and far between in recent years. Although he wrote constantly to all his acquaintances who lived there, he hated to see how the city he associated with the court of King Charles had been transformed into Cromwell's seat of power.

'But, Father, do you really think you need to go? After all, Thomas looked after them well enough on the way here.'

'He was lucky. The number of thieves and highway robbers seems to be growing all the time.'

'But what will you do when you get there?'

Her father, unused to opposition, stared at her indignantly. 'Are you questioning my decisions? I thought Mistress Hawkins was your friend, that you would be pleased that I am going to protect her. I still have friends in London who will be glad to see me and who will accommodate me. Now, will you please go and make sure that I have all that I need for the journey.'

Anne curtseyed and left the room, biting her lip. She knew Sir Edward had grown fond of Lucy, but he really did seem over-anxious about her safety.

Sir Edward's decision caused yet

more upheaval and delay, and Thomas had been at March House for a whole week before everything was ready. An hour before the coach was supposed to leave, Anne was summoned from the kitchen where she had been trying to comfort Bella and Martha who had become fast friends and did not want to be separated. Sir Edward was in his library, already dressed for the journey. He pushed a sheet of paper across his desk casually.

'This requires your signature, Anne.'

She picked up the document and began to read it, but Sir Edward interrupted her.

'There's no need for that! Your signature is just a formality. Sign it and let us go.'

But some words had caught Anne's eye, and she ignored her father and read on carefully. When she came to the end she laid it down on the desk and looked at Sir Edward, her face white.

'You want my permission to sell my mother's jewels.'

'Yes,' he said flatly.

'But they are mine! She left them to me!'

'And now I want to sell them. Sign the paper.'

'No! Everything else is yours, but my mother's jewels are mine, my dowry!'

Mentally she added, 'And if your incompetence brings us to ruin, at least I will have control over something with a little value.'

Sir Edward's heightened colour showed his anger. 'What is the point of a dowry if nobody wants to marry you?' he demanded brutally. 'It is clear that John Haversley wants Lucy, not you, and there is no-one else. Sign!'

Anne shook her head. She had lain awake too many times, worrying about her father's extravagance, grateful that at least he could not sell the small boxful of necklaces and brooches that her mother had left her.

Suddenly Sir Edward collapsed into the chair behind his desk, his hands covering his face. When he lifted his head and looked at his daughter all the arrogance and anger had gone. He looked like a frightened old man.

'Please, Anne,' he whispered. 'There is nothing else I can do. I must sell the jewels.'

'Why?'

He looked down at the desktop, his hands fidgeting with the sheet of paper. 'Lawyer Hawkins has not only been my solicitor. He has lent me money. Now he says it is time I started to pay him back.'

Unsteadily Anne felt for a chair and sat down, gazing at her father. 'So that is why you let Lucy come here! He has power over you.'

'I couldn't refuse him. Over the years he has made various loans to me. I didn't realise how they had added up, and anyway I thought something would happen to restore our fortunes . . . I can't repay all I owe, but if I sell the jewels I can give him something. Would you rather lose March House?'

Anne was thinking desperately.

'So this is why you are going to London, not to protect Lucy.'

'I will be protecting her, but — he ordered me to go to London and I have no choice. Anne, please sign and let me sell the jewels!'

She felt sick. He had left her no choice. She picked up the pen, dipped it in the inkwell, and scrawled her name on the document. As soon as she had finished, her father seized the paper and stood up.

'It is the right thing to do, Anne! I will get a good price for them and it will solve all our worries!'

Already the colour was returning to his face. Anne nodded, avoiding his eyes. She knew her father too well. And ready money would soon vanish and when the next financial crisis came they would face total ruin.

Soon the little group was standing by the carriage where Thomas was already seated, whip in hand. Anne hugged Lucy. Regardless of the relationship between their fathers, she had grown genuinely fond of the younger girl.

'We must meet again,' Lucy insisted. 'Why couldn't you come to London with your father?'

Anne shook her head. 'Someone has to stay here and look after March House. But we will meet again — I am sure of it!'

Then John Haversley appeared clutching a nosegay of rosebuds which he presented to Lucy, and he announced his intention of escorting the coach on its way for the first few miles. Bella and Martha parted reluctantly, and then all that was left was for Anne to say farewell to her father. He came to embrace her with a smile, but his eyes were pleading.

'I'm sorry, Anne,' he whispered as he held her, 'but what else could I do? Forgive me!'

She could not part from him on bad terms and forced herself to smile. 'I understand. There is nothing to forgive. You are doing what you think is best for both of us.'

He looked relieved, and soon the coach, escorted by Sir Edward, Joseph, and John Haversley, rolled down the drive and out of sight.

Anne's shoulders drooped. Her father would probably be away for two or more weeks. She would be lonely without him and Lucy, and she wondered how well she and Martha would eat without Joseph's contributions to the pot.

That evening she told Martha that she would eat with her in the kitchen.

'I'm not going to sit by myself in that enormous dining room when we have a snug kitchen I can share with you,' she said gaily.

Martha looked relieved. 'I'll be glad of your company, Miss,' she confessed. 'It will be lonely without Bella and Joseph.'

Anne enjoyed the cosy little supper, though looking round at the kitchen she did wonder if she would ever reach a point where the kitchen and not the dining room would be considered her natural place. If the worst came to the worst and she had to leave March

House, she would not let her pride stand in the way of earning a living. In these hard times other gentlefolk had become farmers or servants to luckier men. Why should she be any different, especially now marriage to John Haversley was definitely out of the question?

This fact was emphasised when he appeared at March House some days after Lucy and Sir Edward had left. He was dressed in travelling clothes and riding boots, with panniers slung across his horse.

'I've come to say goodbye, Anne,' he announced. 'There are some affairs that need seeing to with our man of business in London, and my mother has asked me to go there and deal with them.'

Anne's eyebrows rose. She wondered how long it had taken him to persuade his mother to let him go. However, she said simply, 'Give my love to Lucy.'

John reddened and then grinned, 'I will,' he promised.

Two days later it was Peter Staunton's turn to take his leave. 'I'm off to

France. I can rely on my head man to look after the Grange.'

'How long are you going for?'

'Some months. I'm hoping to buy more land there, but the negotiations are tricky, and when it's mine I'll have to see it cultivated to my satisfaction.'

She sighed. 'So Martha and I will be left by ourselves.'

'John will call sometimes.'

'Don't you know? He's gone to London as well.'

Peter demanded to be told all about this unexpected event, and then looked thoughtful.

'I suppose this means he is serious about Lucy Hawkins. Well, I'm, not surprised.' He turned to her, frowning. 'If I'd known this I would have put off going to France until your father was back, but now all the arrangements are made.'

'I thought you had a better opinion of me. Martha and I can cope for a few weeks.'

Peter still looked worried. 'If you do

need help, send for my head man. I will instruct him to give you any aid you need.' He paused. 'Anne, you are not happy. Is something worrying you?'

She shook her head, but he persisted.

'Has your father done something to concern you?'

She was sorely tempted to tell him about her mother's jewels. It would be a relief to tell him everything and he could be relied on to reassure her, to make her feel better, but she could not betray her father's stupidity to anyone, so she rapidly changed the subject, asking him about the land he hoped to buy.

When he left Anne thanked him sincerely for his offers of assistance and stood waving goodbye till he was out of sight. Suddenly she realised that she would miss him more than any of those who had gone off to London. Was it because he was such a good friend, or were her feelings growing deeper? It was an uneasy thought.

Peter Staunton was a rich man, but

would he take on a bride who had not only lacked a dowry but also brought with her the burden of Sir Edward and his extravagance? Anyway, Peter had never shown any feeling but friendship for her, so there was no point in brooding, she told herself.

5

At first the time passed pleasantly enough. Free from Sir Edward's expectations and demands, Anne and Martha cleaned and tidied many rooms in the house, and Anne even had time to cultivate her flowers as well as keeping Joseph's vegetable patch tidy. She received a note from her father informing her briefly that Lucy had returned safely to her father and that all was going well. This was reassuring, but then there was silence that stretched out until Anne realised that it was a full month since her father had left March House.

She could not contact him because she had no idea where he might be staying in London and could scarcely write to ask Lawyer Hawkins if he knew her father's address. Probably he had sold her mother's jewels, paid the lawyer whatever he demanded, and been left with a few guineas in his pocket, in which case she assumed he would have been unable to resist the temptation to look up old friends, playing the wealthy country gentleman and boasting about his estate as if March House still kept its former grandeur. He would come back when the money was all gone.

Major Wolford called one morning, ostensibly in his official capacity to see that no problems had arisen in her father's absence. Recent changes by Cromwell had given the military even more power and she took care not to offend him, assuring him that all was well but trying to convey as politely as possible that there was no need to keep a check on her.

A week later, however, she was dismayed to see him riding up the drive again, accompanied by two of his soldiers, but as soon as he was close enough for her to see his face she knew that this was not a courtesy visit. Anne met him at the door and he dismounted quickly and bowed.

'Ma'am . . . ' He did not seem to know how to continue, and she waited, her heart beat uncomfortably fast. Drawn by curiosity, Martha stood behind her.

'Mistress March, I have bad news,' he continued at last, speaking rapidly as if to get his task over as soon as possible. 'Your father, Sir Edward, was attacked by highwaymen on his journey back from London. They killed him.'

Anne did not know if she made a noise or not, but Martha broke into a shrill wail.

'Joseph! What has happened to him?'

'His servant was injured, but he is alive. He will recover.'

Anne went to speak, to ask for information, but suddenly she felt weak and giddy, about to fall. Major Wolford leapt forward to catch her in his arms and he and Martha supported her into the morning room where she sank into a chair and closed her eyes while they stood looking helplessly down at her. After a while she breached deeply, opened her eyes and looked up at the major.

'Tell me what happened.'

It was a common enough tale for those days when many deserters from Cromwell's army and survivors of the broken Royalist forces had turned to robbery as a way of surviving. On the first day of his journey back to March House, Sir Edward and Joseph had been riding along the dusky, deserted roads when suddenly a musket ball from the hedgerow had killed Sir Edward's horse under him before two men challenged them.

Sir Edward had refused to submit quietly to the robbery and had reached for the pistol he carried, only to be cut down before he could draw it. The second robber had fired his musket at Joseph when he tried to come to his master's assistance, wounding him in the leg. A party of travellers a short distance behind had heard the shots and spurred their horses to the rescue but the robbers had fled, leaving Sir Edward dead on the ground and Joseph bleeding heavily.

'What happens now?' Anne said tremulously. 'Where is my father? I must fetch him home.'

Major Wolford was recovering his composure. 'Arrangements have been made. His body is being brought back here.'

'And my husband?' Martha said sharply.

'He is coming as well.' Major Wolford turned back to Anne. 'Is there anything I can do?'

She shook her head. 'Thank you, but I don't know. I need time to think.'

'Then I will leave you for now, but send for me at once if you need assistance.'

When he and his soldiers had ridden away, Anne still sat for some time, only vaguely aware of Martha's sobs and disjointed speech. Guiltily she remembered how peaceful March House had felt without her father; but now suddenly it seemed empty. Finally she stirred herself.

'Life has to go on, Martha,' she said dully. 'The chickens and pigs need feeding, and there is bread to bake.'

For the next twenty-four hours the two women kept themselves busy with domestic chores that stopped them brooding too much on what had happened and what the future might hold. Then Sir Edward came home on a farm cart with a grey-faced Joseph huddled beside the cheap, roughly made coffin. There could be no lying in state, no funeral feast, for the last male member of the March family.

The Puritan minister appeared, offered Anne brief, insincere condolences, and appointed a time for a funeral. On a wet, windy morning, Sir Edward's remains were laid to rest by the church where his ancestors had worshipped. Few people attended the funeral. Sir Edward had not been well known or particularly liked by the local people, who thought he had given himself unjustifiable airs. Peter Staunton was still in France, and in spite of his protests Martha had insisted that Joseph should stay in his cottage and nurse his wounds.

Mistress Haversley appeared for the funeral, and Anne was surprised to see her son beside her. He hurried to speak to Anne.

'Anne, I only got back from London last night. My mother told me what had happened. If I'd know, believe me, I would have come sooner.'

After the service Mistress Haversley left as soon as politeness allowed, although her son assured Anne he would come to see her. Soon Anne and Martha found themselves the only two beside the new-made grave.

'Go back to Joseph, Martha,' Anne said quietly.

'Are you sure? It doesn't seem right to leave you alone.'

'I want a chance to say goodbye to my father by myself.'

Martha hurried away back to her husband and left Anne staring down at the grave. More than anything, she was glad that she had parted from her father on good terms. It was not his fault that politics and religion had disrupted his life.

He was not the only man who had failed to cope with the violent changes that had culminated in the civil war, the execution of King Charles, and the Commonwealth. He had died a lonely, impoverished man, without even a son to carry on his name.

At least she could do one last service for him. Cromwell had forbidden the use of the old Church of England prayer book, and the Puritan minister's short service had lacked grace and comfort. Now, left on her own, Anne drew out a copy of the forbidden prayer book and read the funeral service aloud over her father's dead body.

'*Man that is born of woman hath but a short time to live, and is full of misery. He cometh up, and is cut* down, *like a flower; he fleeth as it were a shadow, and never continueth in one stay. In the midsts of life we are in death.'*

She read steadily to the end, the words bringing comfort. Finally she closed the book, shut her eyes and said farewell to her father. Only then, as she turned away from the fresh grave, did she see Major Wolford standing some yards away, bareheaded in the rain, watching her. For a moment she wondered whether he would challenge her for reading out the forbidden service, but instead he approached her courteously.

'Let me escort you back to March House.'

Her refusal was instinctive. 'There is no need.'

His lips tightened. 'Sir Edward and I disagreed on many things, but I knew he would agree that his daughter should not be left to walk home alone from his funeral.'

She could not argue with this, and

without further words she turned towards the familiar path that led back to March House. Major Staunton walked behind her, as silent as she was. When they reached March House she thanked him.

'You were right. It was a comfort to have someone with me when I left him in the churchyard.'

For a moment she wondered whether he would expect to be invited into the house, and her heart sank at the thought. She was in no condition to make polite conversation, but to her relief he simply bowed.

'I will leave you to grieve now.'

For the first time, gratitude made her feel some warmth towards him.

John Haversley appeared in the early evening. His sympathy and shock at the way her father had died were obviously sincere and heartfelt, but it was not long before he was discussing his own affairs.

'I am home for a few days only. I have decided that a knowledge of law is useful to any landowner in these uncertain times, and I came to tell my mother that I have decided to stay in London for some months to study law there.'

'Does this decision have anything to do with Lucy Hawkins?' Anne enquired.

He had the grace to blush. 'I have visited Lucy several times, and she asked me to give you and your father her best wishes. She will be very distressed to hear what has happened.'

He took his leave soon afterwards, saying that she must be tired after her father's funeral, and she was too proud to ask him to stay and keep her company a little longer.

It was time for Anne to turn her attention to her future. She had a small store of ready money that she had carefully accumulated and kept secret from her father, and Joseph had handed over to her some money that Sir Edward had given him to pay their bills on the journey.

A search of Sir Edward's blood-soaked clothes had revealed a soft leather purse with a small stock of guineas. When Anne had taken these out to count them she had felt something else in the bottom of the purse. It was a string of pearls. She had stood with it in her hand for some time as memories came flooding back. Her mother had told her many times how Sir Edward had given her the pearl necklace after the birth of their daughter, and even though he had been desperate for every penny, Sir Edward had obviously been unable to part with this love token. She closed her fist over it. Whatever else had to go, she would keep this.

Anne also made a far less welcome discovery. Her father had carried documents showing how much he had paid to Lawyer Hawkins and how much he still owed. The remaining debt seemed enormous to Anne and it was clear that the only way she could repay it would be by surrendering March House and its remaining lands to the lawyer.

She went around in a daze, wondering how long it would be until he called in the debt. Then a bundle of papers arrived which she opened with shaking hands. The first document she saw was a letter from Lucy, full of sorrow and sympathy, but the second document was a letter from Lawyer Hawkins. In emotionless, formal language, it regretted the death of her father, and then went on to say that in view of this sad event he would not for the foreseeable future be pressing her to repay the remainder of her father's debts.

The rest of the documents were notes signed by Sir Edward acknowledging loans that were still outstanding. She wondered what the lawyer meant by 'the foreseeable future'. At the moment she could not think of any way of ever possibly repaying him.

Then Mistress Haversley arranged to rent a couple of fields of pasture from her, though she offered the minimum payment, and Anne, when she had checked all the money and resources left to her, calculated that she could survive at March House till the following spring, although she knew that any unexpected bill, such as a demand for taxes, would put her in an untenable condition. Anne knew she was only postponing difficult decisions.

She did not know what would happen when spring arrived and her money ran out. She had no relatives close enough to feel obliged to take in a penniless young woman and Mistress Haversley had contrived to make it clear that she felt no responsibility towards her. Well, she would deal with that when the time came. Meanwhile, she had to think of Martha and Joseph as well as herself.

Apart from her bedroom, the morning room and the kitchen quarters, March House was now shut up. There were stocks of wood for firing from the estate, vegetables and fruit, chicken and eggs. The trouble was that all these resources were running down. Joseph had recovered from his wound, but showed no intention of taking up his old activities. Instead he sat huddled by the fire, rarely speaking.

'His spirit is broken,' Martha said sadly. 'He saw himself as Sir Edward's bodyguard, and then, when the test came, he failed and Sir Edward died. He feels responsible for his death.'

'But it wasn't his fault!'

'He's alive and Sir Edward is dead. He can't forgive himself that.'

Joseph began to show marginal signs of improvement, cleaning his guns and talking about shooting some birds for the pot. One bright autumn day Anne and Martha came back from picking apples to find that he had gone, and so had his old fowling piece. When he did not return they roused the villagers to look for him, and in the early morning light his body was found.

'The gun must have gone off by accident,' Anne insisted to the Puritan minister. 'He had not used it for some time. He must have been careless.'

She could not bear the thought of

Joseph being judged for suicide, for then he would have to be buried in unconsecrated ground, another blow for Martha, but this time the minister and the magistrate who enquired into the death showed mercy and Joseph was allowed to rest near his master.

Then, one morning, Peter Staunton burst into the house like a hurricane and enveloped her in his arms.

'That stupid man of mine!' he raged. 'He sent me a packet of papers, including news of what had happened, and scrawled the direction so badly that it was two months before they reached me. As soon as I received them and learned what had happened to your father I abandoned everything and came back to England. My poor dear!'

Shaken by his sudden appearance, warm in his arms, Anne's defences vanished and she wept for the first time since Sir Edward died. She wailed broken, incoherent words while scalding tears ran down her cheeks until her grief was spent and she stood for the second-time, red-eyed and sobbing, with her head against his chest.

'I missed you!' she said savagely. 'I needed you.'

He hugged her to him like a child, murmuring soothingly, until she had recovered enough to sit in a chair and sip a mug of warmed wine provided by a very alarmed Martha. She gave him an account of what had happened, leaving out the reason why Sir Edward had gone to London.

'So you and Martha are by your-selves,' he said at the end. 'How are you managing?'

'At the moment, well enough, but I'm not sure how well we will cope when winter really comes.'

He nodded thoughtfully. 'I'll leave orders that regular supplies of meat and other foods are to be brought to you regularly.'

She sat up. 'What do you mean? Why do you have to leave orders?'

He thumped the kitchen table mood-ily with his fist. 'I've got to go back to

France, Anne. I had to come to see if you were all right, but there is unfinished business I must see to in France.'

The news dismayed her, but she smiled up at him bravely. 'Thank you for coming.'

He stood up, prepared to leave. 'What else could I do?'

The following morning he sent over a cart piled high with welcome supplies together with a message that he would be calling later. After everything had been unloaded, Martha stood chatting to the carter for some time before she came in, chuckling.

'I'm grateful for what Master Peter has sent, but according to William there he can spare it. He's doing very well for himself in France is our Master Peter!'

'What do you mean?'

'Well, there's some good land next to what he already owns. A young woman who can't run by it herself has inherited it. He's bought some of it, but William says the young lady is eager to marry him and bring him the rest as her dowry, and Master Peter seems willing.'

Anne dropped the cheese she had been holding. 'Stop wasting your time in idle gossip, Martha! We have all this to put away safely.'

Furiously she packed bundles on to the pantry shelves. So Peter Staunton had a wealthy heiress waiting for him in France, and what he felt for Anne was pity, not love! Well, she had her pride!

When Peter arrived later, Anne, on her dignity and very much Mistress Anne of March House, thanked him for what he had sent, but told him there would be no need for further deliveries.

'We are not beggars in need of charity,' she said with icy sweetness.

'But yesterday . . . '

'Yesterday I was not expecting to see you. I overreacted.'

Peter soon left. He called briefly once again, but only to take his leave before returning to France. After he had gone she cried again, secretly and miserably.

6

Life settled into a kind of rhythm, though not a very comfortable one. Looking back, Anne could see how her life had changed dramatically for the worse over the year. In spring she had been the mistress of March House, looked up to as the daughter of Sir Edward March, living a life that at least echoed that of a member of the landed gentry. Now she kept warm in a corner of the house, leaving the rest to rot while she and Martha contrived to live on what they could find. She even found herself thinking wistfully of the rabbit stews she had once despised.

As the weather grew worse, she was grateful for the stores which Peter Staunton had sent and began to think she had been very foolish indeed to refuse his offer of more. Food was more important than pride.

She was chopping wood in the stables one frosty morning, wearing one of her father's coats for warmth, when Major Wolford rode into the yard. When she saw him she dropped the axe and stood up, as if distancing herself from such manual labour, at the same time wondering why he had come.

He was in no hurry to speak, however, looking at her in the old coat till she felt herself blushing. She was not ashamed of her situation, and if it had been John Haversley or Peter Staunton who had called she would have laughed at her dishevelled appearance, but there was something in Major Wolford's cool regard which made her uneasily conscious of how critically others would view her present life.

'You wished to see me, sir?' she said finally.

'Indeed I do,' he replied, dismounting and tying his horse's reins to a post before he turned back to her with the careful politeness he always showed her. 'What I want to discuss with you will take some time. May we go indoors?'

She had no choice but to lead him into the house, aware of his appraising gaze as he looked around the entrance hall and noted the signs of neglect. The morning room was tidy but cold, for all available firewood was now kept for the kitchen for heating and cooking. Anne had discarded her coat in the hall and tried not to shiver in the chill air as she waited for Major Wolford to tell her why he had come. He did not broach the matter immediately.

'I am afraid life is hard for you now your father is gone, Mistress March,' was his first comment.

'Martha and I have everything we need,' she said briskly. The last thing she wanted was sympathy from this man.

'Enough to keep you fed and a roof over your head, perhaps, but certainly not enough for you to live as you have been accustomed to.'

This was getting too personal!

'That is my affair!' she snapped. 'It is

nothing to do with you. Why are you here?'

His lips tightened angrily, but then he forced a smile. 'You are mistaken. I am here to offer you a way out of this misery.' He drew a deliberate breath and then said with great formality. 'Mistress March, I am here to ask you if you will do me the honour of marrying me.'

At first she thought she must have misheard him, but as he stood impassively waiting for her reply she could not help an incredulous laugh and she saw his face twitch.

'You are asking me to marry you?'

'Yes.'

'But I don't even know you!' She forbore to add that she didn't like what she did know.

'We have not spent much time together, but I can assure you that I have learned a great deal about you from the people of the neighbourhood, who hold you in high esteem.'

She had to accept that he was

serious, and with an effort she gathered her thoughts together to make a suitable reply.

'Major Wolford, you have done me a great honour, but I am afraid that I cannot accept your proposal.'

He sighed. 'You are obviously surprised, but I think you should take time to consider before you give me your final reply.'

'Major Wolford, I do not need time to think. I will not marry you!'

'You are already beginning to suffer hardship. This house is cold and damp and beginning to smell of decay. I was not a born gentleman, but I can give you the comfortable existence you used to have. I can restore this house.'

'This house will not be mine for long. It is security for a debt I cannot pay. If you are hoping to marry an heiress, you must find someone else.'

His face twitched in a half-smile.

'Don't be naïve, Mistress March. I know how reckless your father was with money and I guessed that he must have left debts, but I have power. No creditor with any sense will foreclose if I don't want him to. I will pay off some of the money, come to an accommodation, but I can promise you that March House will not be seized if you marry me.'

His voice was as calm as ever, with no trace of the emotion to be expected from a man who is being rejected by the woman he wants to marry. Anne hesitated and gave him a sharp look.

'Why do you want to marry me?' she said curiously. 'You don't love me and I can't believe you are proposing to me out of pity.'

For the first time his smile seemed genuine.

'No, of course I don't love you, and I'm certainly not prepared to offer marriage just to rescue a gentlewoman who has fallen on hard times. Let me be frank. This is a business proposition. Shall we sit down and discuss the matter?'

They sat facing each other across a

small table and Anne eyed him warily as he leant towards her.

'The war and its aftermath have given many an intelligent man opportunities to prosper,' he began. 'The confusion and the change of regime meant that chances could be exploited, and few people dare challenge the actions of a man with a sword who claims he has the authority of Cromwell behind him. I have managed to accumulate a considerable amount of money over the past few years. Unfortunately Cromwell's administrators are too efficient.

'If I bought an estate, for example, they would soon be asking where I got the money. Some unfortunate incidents might be uncovered. But if I marry you people will just assume that your father must have left you better off than they thought when I begin to spend my money. There will be no inconvenient enquiries.'

'And what do I get in return for concealing your crimes?' Anne enquired in a voice which she struggled to keep under control.

He looked at her impatiently. 'I told you. I will restore this house to its proper condition, and you will once again be able to live properly as the mistress of March House. You will have security. I'll even let that old woman servant go on living in her cottage.' He stood up and looked around him and his voice rose triumphantly. 'My father worked on the land every day of his life, serving a master who took his labour for granted while he lazed about in his big house, I swore that one day I would own such a house, that I would have servants and they would obey my orders. When I marry you I will be master of March House, and my children will be gentlefolk! My dream will come true.'

Anne sprang to her feet.

'No! Forget your dream or find someone more desperate than I am. I will never marry a thief, a man I detest!'

Her vehemence took him back

momentarily, and then he shook his head impatiently.

'Don't be a fool! I've seen how you are living. In a few months, when the taxmen come calling, you won't be able to pay. What will you do then?'

'I don't know, but I do know that I will not marry you. Now go!'

His face was convulsed with fury. 'You're as big a fool as your arrogant, half-witted father. You think you're too good for anyone who wasn't born to be a gentleman.'

'Get out!'

He strode towards the door, then swung round and came back to stand menacingly close to her.

'I'll be back. I'll wait till the snows come and you've run out of the little food you have, till the rain starts coming through the roof and you can't keep warm any more. Then you'll be glad to marry me, though I'll make you pay for the way you are treating me now!'

Then he was gone, slamming the

door furiously behind him, and Anne could find relief in tears.

It looked like being a hard winter. Anne and Martha spent most of their time in the kitchen simply trying to keep warm, and had little contact with neighbours or the villagers. Anne had hoped that from now on Major Wolford would avoid her, but a fortnight after she had refused his proposal he rode up to the house. Anne met him at the door, for she was determined not admit him to March House.

Without dismounting he asked her simply, 'Have you changed your mind? Will you marry me?'

'No,' she replied, and he rode off without another word.

But he came a fortnight later with the same question, and received the same reply. Every two weeks the little scene was replayed.

In early December, after one such visit, when frost had gripped the countryside for days, Anne found that the door to the outhouse where their root vegetables were stored had been forced open and the protective straw pulled off. At least half the vegetables were frostbitten and useless.

Martha, who showed little curiosity about anything nowadays, noticed the major's regular visits.

'Why does he come here?' she asked one evening. 'Is it just to make sure we are all right?'

Anne shook her head. 'You won't believe why he comes. He wants to marry me!'

She expected the old servant to react with surprise and then ridicule the major's aspirations, but instead Martha sat up, a light appearing in her dull eyes.

'He wants to marry you? But that would solve all our problems!'

Anne stared at her disbelievingly. 'Martha, you can't want me to marry him! He is a soldier of Cromwell's, a Puritan who represents everything my father hated and fought against.'

'The Puritans rule the country and

Sir Edward is dead. Major Wolford has power, and he seems to have money as well.'

'Martha, I hate the man.'

The servant looked at her sourly. 'What would you rather do? Marry a man you hate or starve to death? Because it seems to me that that is the choice you will have to make.'

'He makes my flesh creep! I couldn't bear to have him near me, or to bear his children!'

'You haven't got the right to be so finicky. Many a woman has had to marry a man she couldn't abide near her, because she didn't have a choice. Anyway, you wouldn't be with him all the time — you would be running the house while he was off carrying out Cromwell's work. You know Cromwell is ruling England through the military now. Major Wolford is going to have a lot of power. You could endure marriage to him if you had to.'

'There must be some other way,' Anne murmured desperately.

'There isn't, Mistress Anne. You say we can manage till spring at the latest. What happens then? Do you think we are going to find a pot of gold or some other miracle is going to save us? Who would take us in once March House was gone?'

Anne had no reply. Once she would have trusted that if the worst came to the worst Mistress Haversley would give her shelter, but she had met the lady on one of her rare visits to church a few weeks previously and had been forced to listen while Mistress Haversley expressed her considerable annoyance because she had been forced to take in an elderly aunt of her dead husband's, a gentlewoman who had fallen on hard times.

'All she does is sit there and eat and complain about her ill fortune. She's living off me like a beggar, yet she still expects to be treated like a lady. I only let her stay because of her connection with my husband.'

Her sharp eyes had been full of

meaning as she stared at Anne and the message was clear. When Mistress Anne March had been the heiress to a comfortable estate, Mistress Haversley had been glad to call her a friend and possibly even consider marrying her son to her, but penniless Anne March could not expect help from her. To change the subject, Anne had enquired about John, and then Mistress Haversley had been all smiles.

'John is doing well. The friendships he is making will stand him in good stead. And, of course, he has seen a great deal of Lucy Hawkins. I understand her father is extremely rich.'

Martha was not prepared to let the subject of Major Wolford drop.

'How do you think Sir Edward would feel,' she said one day, 'if he knew the home he loved was falling to pieces and that you could save it but you are too selfish to do so?'

When Anne stayed silent she tried another approach. 'You may find work when we are thrown out of here,' she complained. 'After all, you are young and strong, and if you want to be a kitchen maid or work in the fields I expect someone will hire you. But you wouldn't be able to earn enough to feed both of us. I will be left to beg my way across England until I'm found dead in a ditch one morning. You could save us both so easily.'

Anne was still silent, but privately she was aware that Martha's arguments were beginning to affect her. Loveless, arranged marriages were common enough between families determined to preserve or enlarge their holdings. Kings rarely met their future consorts till their marriage had been agreed. When she thought what spring might bring, when she considered the possibility of being turned out into the world penniless and friendless, she was very frightened. Did she have the right to consign Martha to a miserable old age because she was so fastidious? Major Wolford could give her security, comfort, and status. All she had to say was 'yes'. No-one else would save her.

She thought of Peter Staunton, and wished desperately that her foolish pride had not sent him away. She remembered the comfort of his arms when she had gone to apologise for her stupidity, the warmth of his body against hers when he had held her briefly in his arms. He would have cared for her and befriended her, even if his heart was given elsewhere. But Peter was in France and there was no word of his return and she cried herself to sleep that night.

Wolford called the next day. It was cold and windy and Anne had spent the morning trying to persuade damp green wood to burn. She was very tired and her eyes were red with smoke. The major looked at her for some time before he spoke, and for a moment she was humiliated by the thought that he might have decided that he did not want such a worn, unattractive woman as his wife.

He leant forward over his horse's neck.

'Will you marry me?'

For the first time she hesitated. He was young, strong, rich and ruthless. It would be so easy to say 'yes', and shed all her burdens. He might not love her, but once she was his property he would fight to protect her, and he would protect Martha as well.

His eyes were bright and fixed on her face as if he sensed her uncertainty.

'Will you marry me?'

She looked at him and thought of his hands touching her, of his lips on hers, and shuddered.

'No!' she shouted and slammed the door shut, then leant against it helplessly as she heard him spur his horse and gallop away. Martha would not speak to her that evening. She wondered if Major Wolford would come again.

Soon it would be Christmas. The Commonwealth had forbidden most of the pagan celebrations that used to mark the season, but Anne was determined that there would be one last good day at March House.

'We'll have roast chicken,' she declared. 'We'll choose one of those who have stopped laying and we'll stuff it with herbs and treat ourselves. There are still a few bottles of wine in the cellar. We'll celebrate Christmas properly!'

Even Martha perked up a little when she heard this.

'There are some oddments of dried fruit in the store cupboards. I'll make us a pudding.'

But a week before Christmas they found that the door to the chicken run had been left open and a fox had got in. all that was left were a few mangled carcasses. Anne and Martha stared at the scene with despair.

'You must have forgotten to bolt the door after you fed them last night,' Martha accused Anne, who shook her head in hopeless denial. She knew that Wolford had done this, or one of his subordinates, just as the major had decreed the destruction of their vegetable store. There would be no chicken for Christmas now. What was worse, there would be no eggs to help eke out their daily diet. Wolford could kill them or save them. Martha was right, she had no choice. Next time Wolford called for her answer, if he did call again, it would have to be 'yes'.

7

'Mistress Haversley invites you, and your maid, to spend Christmas Day with her,' was the message delivered to Anne by a neatly dressed manservant. It was completely unexpected but very welcome.

'Please give Mistress Haversley my thanks, and say we accept her invitation,' Anne replied, and then hurried off to tell Martha the good news.

'So we won't be dining on vegetable soup and scraps of bacon after all,' was the old woman's comment. 'It's not like her to feed people who can't give her something in return,' she added, puzzled.

'Perhaps John will be there. Perhaps he has asked her to invite us. We'll find out when we get there.'

Anne looked forward to the outing as a break in the dismal succession of days. It would also be the last social event she would attend as an unattached woman, because the next time Major Wolford called she would open the door wide, ask him to enter the house, and tell him that she agreed to marry him. She refused to think further than that, to imagine what life with him would be like, and concentrated on convincing herself that Martha was right, that at least it would be better than starving.

On Christmas Day she put on her last surviving good gown and persuaded Martha to arrange her hair becomingly. Wrapped in warm cloaks, the two of them walked to church where the minister preached on suffering and sacrifice and made no mention of rejoicing at the birth of Christ. The congregation was small, as many of the villagers were busy preparing for some form of celebration, though the minister disapproved of such pagan relics. Afterwards Anne and Martha went on foot to the house everybody still spoke of as 'Mistress Haversley's house', ignoring its nominal master, John Haversley.

His mother greeted them with surprising eagerness, ushering Anne into a comfortable drawing room and offering her a glass of mulled wine while Martha went off to join the servants. A small, thin lady who had been enjoying the warmth of the fire was introduced as the elderly aunt. She smiled timidly, bobbed a curtsey, and then retreated to a cosy fireside chair. Mistress Haversley looked at her scornfully.

'All she does is eat and sit by the fire,' she confided to Anne. 'She's no company.'

Anne looked round. 'Is John here today?'

'He hoped to come but then decided that he was too busy in London. Probably Lucy wants him to stay there, and, after all, London has more to offer a young man than a quiet country village.'

She sounded a little depressed, as though she had been trying to persuade herself that these were adequate reasons for her son to leave his mother virtually alone on Christmas Day, and Anne wondered whether Mistress Haversley had invited her because she was feeling lonely. Whatever the reason, it was extremely pleasant to return for a day to her old life as a gentlewoman cushioned by comfort and leisure and waited on by efficient servants.

'What are you thinking of?' Mistress Haversley said curiously as she noted Anne's wistful smile.

'Do you remember Christmas last year? We all celebrated it together at March House — you and John, my father, myself — and Peter Staunton, though my father thought hard before he invited him.'

Mistress Haversley snorted.

'He had no choice! Peter brought plenty of good wine with him — enough for Christmas, New Year, and longer.' Her face fell. 'Our world has changed so much since then. Your father is dead, Peter seems to have decided he prefers France to England, and John is in London. Sometimes I'm afraid that he will decide to live there, and I'll be left here by myself.' She made a visible effort and sat up, smiling determinedly, and raised her glass. 'At least let us enjoy ourselves today, because we don't know what changes next year will bring.'

When they made their way to the dining-room Anne was very impressed. Silver and crystal glistened in the light from the wax candles and the table and sideboard held enough food for a dozen people, let alone the three women who took their seats in a little cluster at one end of the big table and shook out their white linen napkins.

There was roast beef, a great ham, chicken in savoury sauces and elaborate pies and pastries, together with a whole salmon. At a sign from Mistress Haversley, the servant who stood waiting to help them to whatever they wanted poured red wine into their glasses and then filled bowls with soup from the steaming tureen.

The elderly aunt began spooning up the soup eagerly, but before the other two had started the dining room door opened abruptly. Mistress Haversley looked up with annoyance, stared, then dropped her spoon unceremoniously and stood up, pushing her chair back, her arms outspread to greet the figure in the doorway.

'Peter! Come in! Come in! Happy Christmas, my dear!'

Peter Staunton came forward, handing the cloak and hat that had protected him against the winter weather to the serving man. He hugged Mistress Haversley to him and kissed her on both cheeks, releasing her to turn to Anne, who was now advancing to greet him, her hands held out eagerly.

'Mistress March,' he said, bowing, and took one hand and kissed it.

'Don't be so formal. This is Christmas, so kiss the girl properly!' ordered

Mistress Haversley, and Peter bent forward and kissed Anne obediently on the cheek.

'Welcome home, my dear friend,' she murmured, and thought he was about to say something to her, but Mistress Haversley interrupted in order to present him to the elderly aunt, who twittered her greetings but was obviously relieved when they all returned to the table.

'You will eat with us,' the hostess ordered Peter.

'Indeed I will and I shall be delighted to do so, because otherwise there will be no Christmas dinner for me,' Peter informed her. 'I got back from France late last night. No-one was expecting me, so I decided to invite myself to a neighbour's for the feast.'

Everything seemed twice as bright and cheerful to Anne now that Peter was there, and the other two seemed happier as well. He praised the food, complimented Mistress Haversley on her appearance and unobtrusively passed more food to the aunt, who seemed to have an unlimited capacity. He spoke only occasionally to Anne, but from time to time she found him looking at her, and she wondered whether the hardship of recent weeks showed in her appearance. She thought he looked a little thinner in the face and decided that his French heiress had not been looking after him properly.

'What's the latest news?' Mistress Haversley was demanding. 'In this backwater the country could have been invaded by the Dutch or the Spanish and we wouldn't know.'

Peter carved himself another slice of beef. 'I spent a couple of days in Paris recently, and saw Charles Stuart.'

'King Charles the Second,' Anne said firmly, and Peter grinned.

'Well, that's what the Royalists who are in France call him. He certainly doesn't hold royal court, however. He's hard up, living on the generosity of the French king who can't let his cousin starve, but won't fund another disastrous expedition like the one that ended with the battle at Worcester.'

'So you don't think he has any chance of ever really becoming king of England?'

Peter shrugged. 'Who knows? He isn't strong enough to come back using his own power, but his opponents' weakness might give him an opportunity. There have been rumours that Cromwell would like to be crowned king, but he is growing old and his son, Richard, has no liking for power. Charles may get his chance if there is enough confusion after Cromwell's death.'

'What is Charles like?' Anne asked.

'Very different from his parents. He is tall, dark, very ugly and very charming. Women love him, and he has already fathered more than one child.'

Such gossip was a rare commodity, and the women pressed him for details of Paris and the notables he had seen, the interrogation going on after they had returned to the drawing room. Peter had risen from the table with the women, protesting that he was not going to be left to drink his wine alone on Christmas Day.

When there was a momentary silence Anne looked out of the window and realised that dusk had fallen. The aunt was snoring gently in her chair.

'I must go!' Anne exclaimed reluctantly, scrambling to her feet. 'Martha and I will be stumbling home in the dark.'

'The two of you will ride my horse and I will guide you,' Peter stated firmly, also rising. The two of them took leave of Mistress Haversley, thanking her sincerely for her hospitality and she obviously did not want to let them go.

'I have enjoyed your company. The day would have been miserable without you. I would have had to spend Christmas with just that old woman,' she assured them as she kissed them both farewell. Martha had been reluctant to leave the festivities in the kitchen, but was hoisted up behind Anne on the quiet old nag that Peter had ridden. She was clutching a parcel.

'What have you got there?' Anne hissed.

'Just a few pieces,' Martha said, clutching the bundle defensively. 'There's some beef and ham, and a good loaf of bread. There's some crystallised fruit and a chicken as well. After all, the fox got all ours.'

Anne was torn between laughter and distress. 'Martha, we're not beggars.'

'Not yet, but I just dropped a few hints that we would be grateful for any leftovers.'

Anne hoped desperately that Peter could not hear as he trudged along leading the horse by its reins and carrying a lantern. They reached Martha's cottage and saw her safely indoors, still holding on to the parcel, and went on to March House. It loomed dark and unwelcoming. Anne shuddered in anticipation of the damp cold she would encounter inside. Peter halted dubiously.

'I'd better check that all is safe before

I leave you,' he resolved. 'There are too many desperate men roaming the countryside now.' He took her key and went into the house, holding up the lantern, and she saw the flicker of its light as he went from room to room. When he returned he told her that everything seemed secure.

'But lock the door behind you,' he instructed her. 'I'll bid you goodnight now.'

He gathered up his horse's reins, but suddenly Anne felt that she could not let him go so soon.

'Come in with me, Peter. There should still be a fire in the kitchen, and I can give you a glass of that fine brandy you brought my father.'

At first she thought he would refuse and her heart sank, but then he tethered his horse and followed her through the house. The fire was still smouldering on the kitchen hearth and she found a couple of dry logs to put on it and then brought two glasses and the brandy from the sideboard in the dining

127

room where they had been since Sir Edward left for London. She returned to the kitchen triumphantly carrying them to find Peter looking round him grimly.

'What's the matter?'

'The state of this place. It's cold and damp and falling to rack and ruin, and the two of you were glad to get a decent meal and a little food from Mistress Haversley. Anne, you sent me away and refused my offer of help and you gave me the very clear impression that you did not want for anything and that anyway you could get help from Mistress Haversley. What happened?'

'Things change,' she said, handing him a glass of brandy.

'You can explain to me how they have changed tomorrow when I bring you food and firewood,' he said emphatically. 'You can explain why you refused help you knew you needed.'

'Pride,' she said briefly.

'I should have guessed. You are Sir Edward's daughter.' He sighed, and drank some of the brandy. 'Incidentally, from what Mistress Haversley said today, John is courting Lucy Hawkins. Is it true?'

'I think he is doing so with every hope of success. They will make a good couple.' She could no longer keep back the question she had been longing to ask since she had seen him enter the dining room. 'And you? Am I to wish you well on your betrothal?'

He put his glass down abruptly. 'What are you talking about?'

'Martha told me about the heiress whose lands adjoin yours in France, the girl who obviously hoped to marry you.'

'Martha told you?' He stared at her, and then nodded slowly. 'Did Martha tell you that before you rejected my help?'

'Does it matter? Are you betrothed?'

He picked up his glass again and stared into its depths.

'Mademoiselle Varon is a very practical young lady. She thought our combined estates would enrich us both, but when I made it clear that I was not interested she soon shifted her attention to a middle-aged widower whose lands lay on the other side of her estate. I went to their wedding a month ago.'

Anne was silent. She felt very stupid. When she peeped under her lashes at Peter he was grinning. Then he put the glass down yet again and advanced towards her deliberately.

'You were jealous!' he said triumphantly.

'Nonsense!'

He came very close and kissed her.

'No!' she murmured, but found that her hands, instead of pushing him away, gripped his coat and drew him closer. His arms went round her and they kissed again. Finally he swept her off her feet and she found herself sitting on his lap in Martha's roomy chair. For a while they simply held each other silently, and then she sat up a little so that she could look down on him.

'How long have you loved me?' she wondered.

'Ever since the very first time I came back from France.'

'But that's years ago! You never showed any sign of caring for me.'

'What was the use? Everybody said that you were virtually promised already to John Haversley. He was handsome, well bred and rich — an obvious partner for you. And even if there had been no John, think how your father would have reacted if he had guessed how I felt about you. I would have been banned from your presence, whipped off your land if I dared to come near you. All I could do was make sure that I stayed your friend, ready to help you when you needed it and when you allowed me to help.'

It was true. While her father lived there would have been no possibility of him paying her court.

'How long have you loved me?' he asked in his turn.

'I don't know,' she confessed. 'I've only just realised that I do.'

They kissed again, and then he lifted

her to the ground and stood up. 'It's time I went.'

'Stay a little longer!'

'Anne, I love you too much. If I don't go now I will stay the night, and I will not dishonour you.'

It still took some time to say goodnight. Each farewell kiss seemed to lead to another, but finally Peter had mounted his horse and she watched him begin to ride away. Suddenly he pulled his horse's head round and came back to her.

'I forgot one thing, Anne. Will you marry me?'

She laughed.

'Of course!'

'Then I'll see you in the morning.'

Anne huddled in her cold bed, unable to believe that her fortune could have changed so suddenly. She was going to marry Peter Staunton! He loved her! Suddenly she tensed as she remembered Major Wolford. He would not be welcomed into the house next time he came after all, and there was no need to fear him because Peter would protect her. There was nothing to stop them getting married whenever they wished. Presumably they would live in France for part of each year. Peter might even take her to Paris so she could see Charles Stuart, the king in exile.

8

Anne was up early the next morning, cleaning and scouring with energy. She was starting a new life and she wanted everything clean and fresh to match. Peter must have been up early as well, because she heard a cart rumble into the stable yard and a knock on the door even before Martha had appeared. She opened the door and was instantly engulfed in his embrace and kissed heartily. Then he held her away from him and gazed at her.

'I've spent so many years dreaming of being loved by you that I just wanted to make sure last night was real,' he told her. 'Now convince me that it's true,' and she put her arms round his neck and drew him down for another kiss.

An outbreak of indignant squawks interrupted them unromantically and she peered past him at the cart.

'What have you brought?'

'Some decent firewood, flour, butter, cheese, some bacon and ham, and six hens and a cockerel,' he informed her. 'I'd better put the chickens in the chicken run before they start pecking each other.'

Anne watched as he lifted the various objects effortlessly from the cart, noting the smooth flow of his shoulder and back muscles under his shirt, still finding it difficult to believe that she was going to marry him!

There was a groan behind her and she turned to see Martha slowly making her way across the kitchen.

'My head! There was something wrong with the wine yesterday!'

'Or you drank too much. Good morning, Martha!'

A fresh outbreak of cackling from the yard made her clutch her head. 'What is that?'

Anne smiled. 'When my father was betrothed to my mother, he gave her a string of pearls. Now I am betrothed to

Peter Staunton, and he has given me half a dozen chickens.'

Martha stared at her, her headache forgotten. 'You are betrothed to Peter Staunton?'

'We are to be married, yes.'

Martha collapsed into a chair, her hands over her eyes. 'The Lord be thanked!'

'Amen!' responded Anne wholeheartedly.

When Peter reappeared, chicken feathers clinging to his jerkin, Martha scolded him for the awful noise, congratulated him on his betrothal, abruptly collapsed in tears, and was then picked up and kissed by Peter, which made her dissolve in bashful giggles.

Anne and Peter were obviously not going to have the opportunity of any more quiet time together that morning, so Peter retreated to the Grange, leaving Anne to be interrogated.

'You mean all this happened last night after you left me? Master

Staunton never showed any signs of wanting to court you before,' marvelled Martha.

'He couldn't when my father was alive.'

Martha's eyes widened.

'No! I can just imagine Sir Edward's reaction. If he's looking down on us now, let us hope he will forgive you.' She bit her lip and looked cautiously at Anne. 'Well, if you had to choose between Major Wolford and Master Staunton, then I think you chose the right one.'

There was a question in her eyes.

'I didn't choose Peter as the lesser of two evils, Martha! I love him!'

'Then maybe the luck of the Marches has changed at last. Peter Staunton's a fine man and a good man! And we'll never go hungry again!'

Of course the news soon spread after Martha told a few acquaintances in the village and Peter informed his headman, and before long the whole neighbourhood knew.

Mistress Haversley called to congratulate Anne warmly. Anne obviously could have no designs on John Haversley now she was going to be married to a wealthy neighbour. This meant that instead of a penniless girl who might ask favours she was once again a friend worth cultivating.

The following Sunday Peter and Anne attended church together and afterwards received many congratulations from villagers and acquaintances. Anne was standing by Peter's side, listening to an old farmer tell her what a pity it was that her father hadn't survived to hear the glad news, when she looked up to find Major Wolford standing a few feet away. His face was composed, showing no emotion, but his eyes stared at her unblinkingly. Anne gasped and clutched Peter's arm, and he turned to her anxiously.

'What's the matter?' He followed her gaze and saw Major Wolford turn and walk away. 'You're shaking! Are you frightened of that man?'

'Please, take me home,' she managed, and he made their excuses and walked her back to March House while she held his arm tightly. Once there, he insisted on knowing why she had been so upset by the sight of the major, and she had to tell him something of the past.

'After my father died, Major Wolford decided he wanted to be master of March House. He asked me to marry him, and I refused.'

Peter frowned angrily, then looked at her gravely.

'Then that was the end of the matter presumably. Why should he frighten you now?'

She was forced to go on. 'He would not accept that refusal. He came back, again and again.'

She was shivering at the memory of those persistent visits, and gradually Peter extracted the whole story, even the fact that she had been ready to sacrifice herself by accepting the major. His face was very grim, and Anne stretched out an appealing hand.

'It is all in the past now, Peter. You can't do anything to him. He is too powerful, and he has his men to support him.'

'I can't challenge him directly. From what you say of his tactics, he might retaliate in some very unpleasant ways. But you say he wanted March House because it would conceal the way he had got his money?'

She told him what she could remember and he nodded.

'There have been rumours, allegations of threats and blackmail, that people have paid to avoid trouble. One man killed himself and afterwards it was found that his family had been left penniless.'

'Please, Peter, leave him alone.'

He hugged her comfortingly. 'Don't worry, my love. I think he would hesitate before trying to attack me, and now we are betrothed you are under my protection, so there is no need for you to be frightened of him any more.'

Indeed, life did seem to be happy and trouble-free. Food and firewood were once more plentiful at March House and Anne and Peter agreed on a spring wedding.

'I look forward to taking you to France,' he told her. 'My lands are in one of the most beautiful parts of France, and you will have to admit that the weather is better there. My house is of golden stone which glows in the sunlight.'

'March House is beautiful as well. It will be a pleasure to come back here.'

He looked startled. 'But we will not come back here. We will be living at Staunton Grange.'

With a shock Anne realised that she had automatically assumed that they would live at March House. After all, it was a much grander building and her family had lived there for several generations. Staunton Grange was pleasant, but much less impressive. However, Peter was adamant.

'As my wife, you will come to my

home. Anne, this place is becoming a ruin. It may have happy memories for you, but do you really think I want to live in a house where I was received reluctantly at best and often treated as little better than a servant?'

Anne could not think of an answer. She had told Peter about the debt owed to Lawyer Hawkins, but she had blithely assumed that Peter was rich enough to pay off the lawyer and would be willing to do so. Apart from that, she found it difficult to picture herself moving from March House, even in its present state, into unassuming Staunton Grange. Surely Peter could see that?

The question had not been raised again when one morning Martha told Anne that John Haversley had returned home. Anne was very surprised.

'Are you sure he is back? I would have expected him to come to see me.'

'It's not only you he's been ignoring. Apparently he has been back for a good week but no-one has seen him outside his house.'

This seemed odd, and Peter thought the same when he heard the news.

'If he is home, it is his duty out of common politeness to come to see both of us. I will make some excuse to call in.'

Two days later he walked in and announced he had brought a visitor with him. It was John Haversley, but he was no longer the self-confident swaggering young man who had left for London. He was thin and pale, his face haggard, and he kept looking round anxiously.

He congratulated Anne and Peter on their betrothal and apologised for the delay in doing so, explaining that there had been a lot to see to after his long absence. Anne asked after Lucy, and John assured her that she was well, but seemed disinclined to say any more. When Martha bustled in demanding news of her friend, Bella, Peter took the opportunity to draw Anne aside.

'Something is the matter with him, but so far he won't tell me,' he whispered. 'That stuff about having a lot to do was nonsense. His mother runs the place like clockwork. I got the impression that he was scared to leave the house. It took a lot of persuasion to get him to come here, but I told him you would be offended if he didn't come to congratulate us. I thought it might be easier to get him to confide in us away from his mother.'

But neither tactful, probing approaches nor direct questions could get anything from John to explain his behaviour. Exasperated, Peter gave up.

'It's probably one of the usual things that happen to inexperienced young men when they go to a big city for the first time. He has fallen in love with some unsuitable woman or he got involved in gambling beyond his means and now dare not tell his mother,' was his verdict.

'Is that what happened to you in Paris?' Anne challenged him, and he smiled mischievously.

'I never gambled.'

'But you fell in love with unsuitable women?'

'Of course! Every week!'

She made as if to box his ears and he caught her wrist, then let her go as they heard a cry from Martha who was peering out the window.

'Soldiers are coming up the drive!'

Anne and Peter hurried to look out. A small party of half a dozen soldiers was cantering up the drive, but before they reached the house they turned off across the lawns, making for the village. Peter stared after them.

'I think that was a little display for my benefit. Wolford wants to show me that he and his men can go anywhere and do anything they like. I'm not impressed.'

'Where's John?' Anne asked suddenly.

They found their friend huddled on the floor beneath the window in the drawing-room. He was cowering, trying to curl into as small a space as possible. Anne and Peter hurried to kneel by his side.

'What's the matter? What can we do?'

Peter pulled his friend's hands away from his face and forced him into a sitting position.

'No more pretence. You were terrified when you thought those soldiers were coming here. Why?'

'I thought they were coming to arrest me.'

Anne and Peter looked at each other in bewilderment, before Peter too charge.

'Get him some brandy, Anne. We've got to get to the bottom of this.'

When she came back with a glass and a bottle Peter had lifted John bodily and seated him in an armchair. He poured out a generous measure of spirit and almost forced his friend to drink it. After a second glass John was reviving slightly. He looked up at Anne.

'It was all your father's fault,' he said resentfully. 'When I went to London I went to pay my respects to him as a matter of courtesy. He said he could introduce me to men I would find congenial, who thought in the same way as we did. I knew he meant Royalists, but then there are thousands of Royalists still in England, so I went with him to an inn. There was a group of about half a dozen and they welcomed me.

'Afterwards, I couldn't go and see Lucy every evening and I didn't know anyone else in London so I got into the habit of going back to the inn to spend the evening with them from time to time. I didn't see any harm in it.'

His eyes were those of a trapped animal. 'We were all dedicated to the King's cause and of course we all condemned Cromwell and wished him dead.'

There was a long pause. 'But then one of them began to say that just wishing him dead was not enough if we were truly supporters of the rightful King. We should do something. That's when a lot of the group stopped coming to the inn, but I went on.'

He shook his head as if amazed at his

own stupidity. 'Fighting for the King was always such a glamorous and exciting idea, and I wanted to show that I wasn't a coward. It was just an idea at first. We devised a plan, then tried to see if we could obtain the equipment needed to carry it out. Bit by bit, before I realised it, I was drawn into a plot to assassinate Cromwell.'

Peter was muttering curses under his breath as John went on.

'It was planned to ambush Cromwell at a place called Shepherd's Bush. Our leader obtained seven guns, each of which held several balls, so that sheer firepower would cut Cromwell and his guards down and give us time to escape on the horses we had waiting.'

Peter interrupted. 'Your leader — was he Miles Syndercombe?'

John stared at him. 'How did you know?'

'I have heard something of the story. Go on.'

'I was afraid that if I did help in the attempt and it failed I would be seized by Cromwell's men, but if I refused to take part Syndercombe might kill me because I knew too much. Before I could make up my mind it was the day of the attempt and I was put in charge of the horses to make our escape, but when Cromwell was passing by and Syndercombe and others tried to shoot him the guns would not work. Perhaps the mechanism was too complicated.'

He sighed. 'I was so relieved! I thought the nightmare was over and the plotters would give up. Instead, they devised another plan, though this time I wasn't asked to take part.'

Peter's grave voice took up the narrative.

'Syndercombe obtained entry to Whitehall where Cromwell was to sleep on January the ninth. He planned to start a fire and burn the place down. Even if Cromwell wasn't burnt alive he was to be killed in the confusion. Syndercombe got as far as lighting a slow-burning fuse, but one of the other conspirators had betrayed him and he was arrested in Whitehall before any damage was done. A trader told me the story a few days ago.'

Anne shook her head in bewilderment. 'Then there's no reason for John to be afraid. He didn't harm Cromwell and he wasn't involved in the attempt at Whitehall.'

The two men looked at her sombrely.

'You don't understand,' John said bleakly. 'If Syndercombe names me as a conspirator in the first attempt, Cromwell will have me arrested and executed. That's why I came home. I hoped no-one would be able to find me. I should have known better. Cromwell will scour every inch of the country to track down the people who tried to kill him.'

'If Syndercombe does name you, is there any evidence to support his allegations? Are there any letters? Did you put anything in writing?' Peter demanded.

'I had the sense not to do that.'

'Have you told your mother?'

John grew even paler. 'I can't! She would be horrified by what I'd done, and then she'd panic and make such a fuss trying to protect me that it would only attract attention.'

Anne concentrated on soothing and reassuring John, assuring him that no-one was likely to suspect him in that quiet neighbourhood. Peter was silent for some time, pacing about the room, until he stopped and faced John as if he had come to some decision.

'You may be safe here, but we can't be sure. You must go to France.' Both John and Anne tried to speak but he ignored them. 'I have the contacts necessary to smuggle you over the Channel quietly. Once in France you can stay on my estates or you can go to Paris and join the Royalists there.'

John was sitting up, as if he had seen a ray of hope at last. 'Will you really do that for me?'

'Of course, but you must go as soon as possible in case Syndercombe has broken and betrayed you. I suggest you ride over here tomorrow morning, as if you were just coming to pay Anne a visit. Don't bring anything or your mother may guess you are leaving. We will tell her later. I'll meet you and start you on your way.'

John's gratitude was fervent and tearful, and he looked much more like the old self-confident John they remembered when he left for his home. Peter had cautioned him not to say or do anything which might alert Mistress Haversley.

Anne was still uncertain about the plan.

'Is there really any need for him to run away?' she questioned when she was alone with Peter. 'Even if Cromwell's officers did find him and arrest him, they could see that really he's only a boy who got caught up in the plotting accidentally. He is weak and stupid, but he is not a killer.'

Peter shook his head.

'Cromwell knows that his unpopularity is growing and that there are plots against his life. A lot of his time is spent avoiding possible assassination. It's said that he has various bedchambers prepared for him and only decides at the last minute which one he will actually sleep in. He intends to make an example of anyone who is caught and found guilty so as to warn off others. I did not tell John because he was in a bad enough state already, but at the trial of Miles Syndercombe, the leader of the would-be assassins, it was decided that the title of Protector, which Cromwell bears, is in law synonymous with that of king, so that Syndercombe was found guilty of high treason. He has been sentenced to a traitor's death. He will be hung, drawn and quartered.'

Anne felt sick.

'This is a dreadful death!'

'True. But if any of Syndercombe's co-conspirators are caught they will suffer the same fate. Do you want John to die like that?'

'Of course not!' Then an awful

thought struck her and she clutched at his arm. 'If anyone finds out that John was one of the conspirators and that you have helped him escape, you will be regarded as an accessory. You are putting yourself at risk.'

'Of course I realise that, but I must do anything I can to help John. I could not live with myself if he were to be caught and killed when I might have saved him. As you say, he is weak and biddable, but that will not be considered an excuse for his crimes. He is our friend and we must do what we can to save him.'

Reluctantly, Anne had to acknowledge the force of his argument.

'He blames my father for getting him involved,' she said unhappily. 'I can't remember him ever referring to this Miles Syndercombe, but then he was constantly writing to do many people that I didn't know.'

9

John arrived at March House at nine in the morning, though Peter had told him that nothing was likely to happen before noon. He had brought no luggage, as Peter had instructed him, though his pockets were bulging in a way that his mother might have questioned if he had not slipped out before she could see him.

'I should have gone to France years ago,' he told Anne. 'King Charles needs loyal followers around him. I can offer him my sword.'

'From what Peter says, King Charles would prefer money. Have you got any?'

John's face fell at such brutal practically. 'I have some — enough for a few weeks.'

'Then you'd better stay on Peter's estate for a while until we find out whether your mother is able to send you more. At least she will know where you are.'

Anne decided she had been right about John. He was a nice lad, but weak.

'What about Lucy? Do you realise that if you go to France you may never see her again?'

John looked downcast. 'I have thought of that. I wondered whether to risk everything for her and stay in England.' He stared at her miserably. 'I do love her, Anne. Perhaps she could come to France to be with me.'

Privately Anne doubted very much if Lawyer Hawkins would allow his precious daughter to do any such thing, but she patted John's head comfortingly and urged him to eat the food that Martha had prepared before going off to visit a friend, the innkeeper's wife in the village.

An hour later she heard wheels on the drive. Perhaps Peter was early? But when she looked out she was amazed to see a familiar vehicle outside the front door. It was the Hawkins' coach, with Thomas already helping Lucy alight, and before she could open the door she could hear Lucy's fists thumping on the oak panels. When she opened it the girl virtually fell into her arms.

'Where's John?' Lucy demanded without any further greeting. 'Has he come home? Why haven't I heard from him?'

The noise had drawn John to the entrance hall, and when Lucy saw him she abandoned Anne and threw herself into his arms. They held each other tightly while Anne stared first at them and then at Thomas as he carried some baggage into the house.

'Lucy, what are you doing here?' The two young people ignored her and she drew a deep breath. 'Lucy! John!' Startled, they fell apart and stared at her as she stood with her hands on her hips. 'This is my house and I want to know what's going on,' she said crisply. 'The two of you can go in the kitchen and wait for me. I want a word with Thomas.'

Obediently, hand in hand they made for the kitchen while she turned briskly to the driver.

'Now, tell me what your mistress is up to.'

Thomas looked at her despairingly. 'Mistress Lucy has been getting more and more upset because young Master John there seemed to have vanished off the face of the earth. Then the master had to go out of London for a few days and the next thing I knew was that Mistress Lucy was ordering me to bring her down here, I refused at first, saying the master would never permit it, but she said if I wouldn't bring her in the coach she would make her own way here. I knew she was capable of trying to do that, so I thought that at least if I brought her I could tell Lawyer Hawkins that I was making sure she was safe.'

Anne nodded. 'You did the right thing and I shall tell your master so. Now, take the coach round to the stables and look after the horses.'

Thomas, looking relieved now the responsibility for Lucy had been passed to someone else, returned to the coach and Anne made her way to the kitchen where she found Lucy and John waiting for her, both looking very wary. She sat down and looked at them sternly.

'First of all, Lucy, you can explain.'

Eager to defend her strange behaviour, words came pouring out of the young girl.

'John disappeared and there was no message from him. No-one at his lodgings knew where he was, so I guessed if he was still alive he must have come home here so I made Thomas bring me. I didn't know how Mistress Haversley would react if I drove up to her house and then John wasn't there, so I came here first to get any news of him and to see if you could help me.'

John broke in. 'My love, I left London without sending you word because I wanted to protect you, to keep you ignorant of what was happening.'

159

'You mean your involvement with Miles Syndercombe?'

Anne and John were briefly silent with astonishment.

'How did you know?' John asked blankly.

'You mentioned him frequently at one time. You said he was a new friend who shared your views on the state of the country. Then you stopped talking about him, but when I heard about the man who had been arrested when he was trying to burn down Whitehall I remembered the name. Were you one of the plotters?'

'To start with . . . ' John hesitated, and then told her the story that Anne had heard the previous day — how he had been involved in the first assassination attempt but had disassociated himself from Syndercombe afterwards. However, in this version he appeared a nobler person, reluctant to shoot Cromwell from ambush because it seemed a cowardly and ungentlemanly thing to do. 'So I am in danger of being arrested if Miles tells them about me,' he finished.

'No, you are not,' Lucy said extremely firmly.

'How can you know that?'

'Because Miles Syndercombe was found dead in his bed a few hours before he was due to be executed. He had inhaled poison. Cromwell was extremely angry. He wanted Syndercombe to be publicly butchered as a warning to any other possible assassins.'

'And Miles didn't betray his associates?'

'He was described as obstinately silent.'

Anne heaved a sigh of relief. 'You are safe, John. You don't have to go to France after all.'

His face was a mixture of emotions, but he shook his head.

'The main danger died with Syndercombe, but others in the group knew me. If one of them is captured he may not be as stubborn as Miles.' He turned to Lucy and took her hands in his.

'Peter Staunton is going to marry Anne, and he is arranging for me to be smuggled to France today. Come with me!'

Lucy pulled herself free. 'Don't be stupid!'

'I thought you loved me!' her shocked lover pleaded.

'I do, John. But I'm not going to run away to France and spend the rest of my life dragging round the continent in poverty. You can stay in England.' Her voice was brisk and businesslike. 'If any suspicion does fall on you, then running away to France will look like a confession of guilt.'

'Then what can I do?' John almost wailed.

'You can come back to London with me. That is what an innocent man would do. And if there is any trouble, then my father is one of the best lawyers in England. He won't let anyone touch you.'

'Would your father do that for John?' Anne interjected.

'He will if I tell him to,' Lucy said confidently.

It did seem the best plan, the more they thought about it.

'We'll let it be known that you have come to visit me again,' Anne suggested. 'Then in a few days, when you are to go back to London, it will only be natural for John to offer to escort you there while he returns to his studies.'

John looked a little self-conscious, and Anne wondered whether he had actually managed to fit in any study at all. Lucy was delighted with the plan.

'I've missed you!' she told Anne. 'I wanted to come back and see if I could help you after your father was killed, but my father didn't think it was a good idea.' She tucked her arm through Anne's. 'You must tell me what has been happening to you during the last few months, and all about this betrothal to Peter Staunton. I liked him very much. And do you think I could have something to drink, and some food as well, please?'

'Where are my manners? I should have offered you some earlier, and I expect Thomas would like some as well. Peter will be here himself soon.'

All problems seemed to have been solved, and she started to assemble something for them all to eat, reflecting that now Lucy had decided that John was the man for her she would fight like a tiger to protect him. They were settling down to enjoy some refreshments when there was a clatter of footsteps and Martha burst in through the kitchen door. She halted and her jaw dropped when she saw the visitors.

'Mistress Lucy! Then it is your coach in the stable yard!'

Lucy rose and hugged her. 'I am here for a short visit, Martha, though I'm afraid Bella couldn't come this time.'

But Martha was not listening. She had turned urgently to Anne.

'Mistress, there's trouble. Two of Wolford's men were talking in the inn. They said he is bringing a troop here this morning to make an arrest!'

There was a moment when the words did not make sense to Anne, and then she saw that John was white and trembling.

'Someone must have been broken by torture and named the plotters! He is coming to arrest me!' the young man stammered.

'That can't be right. Why should he come here instead of going to your house?' puzzled Anne.

'He must have learned that I plan to go to France, and that I am meeting Peter here.'

Anne went cold. This was what she had feared. John's stupid involvement with the plotters would bring harm to Peter as well.

'I sent the pot boy to Staunton Grange to tell Master Peter what I had heard,' Martha said hurriedly.

'So Peter will have a chance to get away safely,' Anne said thankfully.

'What about me?' John said, on the point of collapse.

Lucy was on her feet, looking very

determined. 'Martha, tell Thomas to harness up the horses again at once. I didn't like your Major Wolford when I saw him before, and I won't let him take you now, John. His authority only covers a limited area so if we can get to the town before he catches up with us, he can do nothing, and we shall be well on our way before he can find the man in charge there and try to persuade him to stop us.'

She turned to Anne. 'You had better come with us as well. After all, you know that Peter was going to smuggle John over the Channel. You are an accessory too.'

Martha heard this as she came back from the stable yard and yelped.

'Does that mean I am going to be left here on my own to face the Major?'

'Of course not,' said Lucy, smiling at the old servant warmly. 'You are coming to London with us. Bella will be delighted to welcome you there.'

It meant abandoning everything, but it did seem the sensible thing to do.

Thomas soon had the coach ready and Lucy, John and Martha took their seats. Anne hesitated before climbing in. She stood on the drive and took one last look at the house and gardens, wondering when she would see them again. When she turned back to the coach she saw Thomas was frowning deeply.

'What is wrong?'

The coachman shook his head despondently. 'I am not sure we can beat the troopers to the town, Mistress March. The coach is fully loaded and the horses did not have enough time for a proper rest. They will soon tire.'

Anne stood unmoving for a few long seconds, and then she closed the coach door and smiled in at the surprised occupants.

'I am staying here. You can go faster without my weight, and I can delay the soldiers when they get here. I don't think they can really charge me with anything.'

John gulped and she saw him try to

summon up some resolution.

'I must be the one to stay, Anne. They want me. I don't think they will bother pursuing you.'

Anne saw Lucy grip John's arm anxiously, and she shook her head.

'It would be very suspicious if I ran away and left you to guard March House. Besides, you must protect Lucy and Martha till you get to London. Major Wolford won't dare touch me.'

'Are you sure?' he said anxiously, and she saw the relief on his face.

'She's right! Of course she is right!' Lucy exclaimed impatiently. 'Anne, send us a message as soon as you can and I'll let you know when we are safe in London. Thomas, drive on!'

Thomas, as anxious as his mistress to be home, cracked his whip, and the coach rolled away, leaving Anne standing alone and feeling very lonely.

10

Anne walked slowly back into the house, poured herself a glass of wine and sipped it slowly.

'Whatever happens, I am the last of the March family. I may be only a woman instead of the son my father wanted, but I will be brave when Wolford comes here,' she said aloud, then shook her head in disgust. How pompous she sounded! She would be helpless against the soldiers.

She went into the long-neglected drawing-room and looked round at the portraits of her ancestors which lined the walls. What would they think of her situation? What would they expect her to do? The wine finished, she put down her glass and stood in front of her father's portrait for a while before she moved to the picture of her long-dead mother.

'Would things have been any different if you had lived?' she wondered, but told herself not to be stupid. The portraits were just paint smeared on canvas. They had no message for her and could not comfort her.

Restlessly she walked up and down on the faded carpet, waiting for the next stage in the drama. Finally, just as she was deciding that Martha must have made a mistake about Wolford's plans, heavy blows thudded on the main door and she knew that the major and his men had arrived. She drew a deep breath, smoothed down her dress, and with head held high walked slowly to the door.

Outside Major Wolford and four of his soldiers waited astride their horses. Their helmets and steel breastplates made it clear that this was no courtesy call.

'Mistress March,' Wolford greeted her harshly, 'I am here to arrest you and to convey you to prison.'

He was here to arrest her, not John?

'On what charge?'

'You are charged with high treason, with plotting to assassinate the Lord Protector of English, Oliver Cromwell.'

There was something dreadfully wrong! The only thing of which she could possibly be accused was of aiding John Haversley to escape.

Anne laughed uncertainly. 'You know that I have not left March House for the past five years. How could I plot such an assassination? What grounds have you got for such an unlikely charge?'

She received a smile that was more like a snarl. 'I have been informed by those investigating the affairs of the traitor, Miles Syndercombe, that they found several letters at his lodgings from your father, promising his assistance in any attempt to remove Cromwell from power, and assuring Syndercombe that his family, which means you, agreed with him.'

Everything seemed to whirl around Anne, and she gripped the doorjamb to keep herself upright. Her poor, silly, silly, stupid father!

'My father spent many hours writing to people he hardly knew or had never met,' she said disdainfully. 'Everyone knew he hated Cromwell. He talked a lot about what he thought should be done, but he never did anything.'

'Nevertheless, we have his letters calling for Cromwell to be killed, written to a man who made two attempts to assassinate the Lord Protector,' Major Wolford said dismissively.

He gestured to his soldiers. 'Search the house.' He grinned ferociously. 'You know what you have to do.'

As the four shouldered their way past Anne and into March House, Wolford himself dismounted and came close, looming over her triumphantly.

'You know no court will uphold these charges against me!' she told him.

'That is probably true. I also know that it can take a long time for such a case to come to court, and I am afraid that prisons are uncomfortable places for gentlefolk. Conditions can be unbearable for those whom the gaolers dislike. Often prisoners have to rely on friends for such basic necessities as food, and gaol fever kills many before they come to trial.'

'Master Staunton will not stand idly by and let me be imprisoned on such trumped-up charges.'

He shrugged. 'You have been accused of treason and even Master Staunton may not be able to gain access to you in a secure prison. I do not think he will ever see you again.'

And Peter by this time would be on his way to France, convinced that he was in danger, not her. She might be dead before he learned the truth.

'You mean for me to die in prison,' she said flatly.

'Yes,' he said curtly.

They stood silently waiting for the soldiers to reappear, and she could hear bangs and crashes as they made their way through the house. One, then two, windows shattered as musket butts struck at them. Finally the troopers came out of the house and Wolford gestured to one of them. 'The prisoner will ride behind you.'

Anne was about to resist the order to mount, but she realised that the men would enjoy the opportunity to man-handle her and reluctantly allowed herself to be hoisted up like a sack behind the trooper.

As he gathered up the reins, she thought she smelled smoke, and when she looked at March House she saw through two of the windows that flames were flickering in the rooms.

'Your men have set the place on fire!' she shouted.

Major Wolford laughed as he glanced casually at the house. 'Some embers must have fallen out of the fireplace after we left,' he said.

Anne was raging helplessly as the horses cantered along the drive. The one bright spot was that the coach would have a good head start by now if Wolford wanted to pursue it, though so far he had said nothing about John Haversley. Perhaps Lucy was right, and there was no surviving evidence against him.

There was a sharp bend near the end of the drive as it approached the public highway, designed to hide March House from the gaze of casual travellers. To help achieve this, groves of trees had been planted on each side. As Wolford's little group swung round this bend, Peter Staunton stepped out of the trees and stood in the middle of the drive. Apart from a cudgel, he was unarmed.

Major Wolford reined in his horse abruptly, as did his men.

'Get out of the way, you fool!' Wolford ordered Peter.

'Let Mistress March go.'

'She is a traitor and the daughter of a traitor, and she will die in prison!'

'Let her go,' Peter repeated stubbornly.

Suddenly Wolford drew his heavy cavalry sword and dug his spurs into his

175

horse's side, charging at Peter. Anne screamed, at the same time throwing her arms around the soldier seated in front of her to impede any attempt to go to the aid of his officer. Peter stood unmoving in Wolford's path till the sword swept down to kill him, and then he moved swiftly, the force of his cudgel parrying the sword blade and then striking Wolford on the side of his head.

Already unbalanced as he leant down to strike Peter, Wolford was knocked from his horse, and before he could scramble up Peter had seized the sword and was holding it at Wolford's throat as he sprawled on the ground. The soldiers made to draw their pistols, but Peter held up a warning hand.

'If one of you draws on me, I'll cut your officer's throat.'

It was deadlock, and as the frustrated troopers wondered what to do Anne slid from the horse which carried her and ran to Peter's side.

'Get Wolford's pistol, cock it, and give it to me,' he instructed her, and now he faced his enemies with two weapons, but even with a blade at his throat Wolford sneered up at him.

'You look very brave at the moment, but you are one man against five. Sooner or later your arm will get tired and then my men will have you.'

Peter smiled. 'If I were you I would hope that my arms are strong enough to hold these weapons for some time, because as soon as I feel I am weakening I swear to you I will kill you. Anne, run while you can!'

She did not move. 'I've nowhere to go. I'll stay with you.'

'Run!'

'I don't want to live if you are killed. I'm staying.'

Wolford was silent, and the minutes passed slowly. Anne edged close to Peter.

'We can't stay like this for ever. Is there anything we can do?'

'I'm afraid there is nothing we can do, my love, but I am hoping that other people may come to our aid. Let us hope they come in time.'

More minutes passed, and Anne realised that very slowly, almost imperceptibly, the troopers' horses were drifting closer. Each time an animal fidgeted, it came to a halt a few inches nearer Peter. Soon one of the soldiers might risk charging him. Drops of sweat were running down Peter's face with the effort of holding the sword. A smile crept on Wolford's face, but then Peter shifted position slightly and the sword blade pressed hard against Wolford's neck and the smile disappeared.

Just when it seemed that Peter could not hold out much longer and that the soldiers were ready to risk a desperate rescue attempt, there came the sound of galloping horses, and Anne saw a party of twelve riders coming up the drive from the road. But they were wearing the buff jerkins and distinctive helmets of Cromwell's men!

'You lose! Touch me now and you'll both die in seconds!' Wolford spat out, but Peter seemed unworried, maintaining his grip on his weapons as the newcomers swept up to them and surrounded them. To Anne's amazement, the officer leading them saluted Peter.

'Master Staunton!'

'Colonel Weatherby,' Peter acknowledged, and now he lowered his arms at last as Wolford scrambled to his feet in undignified haste and addressed the colonel.

'I am Major Wolford, the Lord Protector's representative in this area. Seize these two! The woman is a traitor and the man has threatened my life!'

Colonel Weatherby looked at him coolly. 'You admit that you are Wolford?'

'Admit it? I have just told you of my authority here!'

Colonel Weatherby gestured his men forward. 'Major Wolford, I am here to arrest you on suspicion of corruption and theft.'

Wolford and his men were quickly

and efficiently surrounded and his soldiers were disarmed, while Wolford indignantly protested his innocence and Anne took shelter in Peter's arms.

'Such accusations are lies spread by my enemies such as Staunton here!'

Colonel Weatherby sighed.

'We have already spent some weeks investigating your affairs. We have found ample proof of your crimes.' He lifted his head. 'Can any of you smell smoke?'

'The soldiers set fire to my home, March House, when they arrested me,' Anne informed him.

'We were just carrying out our officer's orders!' exclaimed a trooper frantically as Weatherby's face grew grim.

'Another crime to add to a long list!' He turned to where Peter stood holding Anne. 'I must thank you for your help, Master Staunton, and I am relieved that we managed to arrive in time to help you. We will take care of Major Wolford and his men now.' He edged his horse closer to the pair and lowered his voice. 'May I suggest that a temporary absence might be a good idea?'

Then he gathered his men and prisoners together and rode off, Wolford craning round to gaze at them vindictively while still protesting his innocence.

'How did you know the colonel was coming?' Anne enquired shakily.

'I didn't know. I hoped he would. I gathered evidence of some of Wolford's extortions and sent the evidence to his superiors. I knew they were coming to arrest him today, so as soon as I got Martha's message I sent a lad to find them and beg them to hurry because I suspected we would need their help.'

He turned to look up the drive.

'Did you say March House was on fire? Let us go and see what is happening.'

As soon as they rounded the bend they saw that the house was already blazing from end to end.

'They must have started fires in more than one place,' Peter said bleakly.

'Nothing can be saved.' Then his grip on Anne tightened. 'What about Martha? Is she safe?'

Anne began, 'Martha is on her way to London with John Haversley and Lucy Hawkins.' She laughed as he stared at her. 'I can explain.'

Then she looked at her home. The portraits, the furniture, all the memories of her family were being destroyed.

'Don't look,' Peter told her. 'I know how much you loved the place.'

But she gazed steadily as the roof caught fire and began to collapse.

'It is only bricks and mortar and it has served its purpose. I have not been happy there for a long time. Lawyer Hawkins can have the land now to pay off my father's debts. I'm glad to be rid of the burden.'

Then the practical extent of her losses dawned on her. 'Peter! I've got nothing!'

'That doesn't matter, my love. I've got plenty.'

'But I've got absolutely nothing

except the clothes I'm wearing, not even a cloak to keep me warm!'

She was shivering with reaction to the recent danger as well as with cold, but fortunately Peter was good at dealing with practicalities and stripped off his jerkin and wrapped it round her.

'I'll take you to Mistress Haversley. She will have to give you shelter now. It will get your blood moving if we walk fast. Now, tell me about Lucy and John.'

This she did rapidly, and he nodded with satisfaction at the end.

'At least we can tell Mistress Haversley that her son has run away because of love, which is much better than having to tell her that he was a would-be murderer.' He gave a shout of laughter. 'I can almost feel sorry for the lad. With Mistress Haversley as his mother and Lucy Hawkins as his wife he'll never have a chance to call his soul his own.'

Anne stooped. 'You were going to help him get to France today. What has happened about that?'

'The men who were going to take him will wait at the Grange until I get back, but they will be pleased I can tell them they won't be burdened with a runaway. Remind me to send someone to collect the chickens.'

They walked on until Anne queried in a small voice, 'What happens next to us, Peter?'

'You heard Colonel Weatherby. He suggested a temporary absence. Wolford is going to make all kinds of accusations against us to try and distract from the investigation into his affairs, but there won't be much point in his doing that if we are not available for questioning.'

'So?'

'So, my love, we are going to get married as soon as possible, within the next few days, and then I shall take you to France, which, as I have said, you will like very much. The farmer is finally going to marry the gentle-woman.'

'You mean the penniless girl is going

to marry the rich wine-grower!'

He smiled lovingly and bent to kiss her.

'I mean that Peter is going to marry Anne, and they are going to live happily ever after.'

THE END